Welcome to Harlequin's great new series, created by some of our bestselling authors from Down Under:

THE AUSTRALIANS

Twelve tales of heated romance and adventure— guaranteed to turn your whole world upside down!

Travel to an Outback cattle station, experience the glamour of the Gold Coast or visit the bright lights of Sydney where you'll meet twelve engaging young women, all feisty and all about to face their biggest challenge yet...falling in love.

And it will take some very special women to tame our heroes! Strong, rugged, often infuriating and always irresistible, they're one hundred percent prime Australian male: hard to get close to...but even harder to forget!

The Wonder from Down Under:
where spirited women win the hearts of
Australia's most independent men.

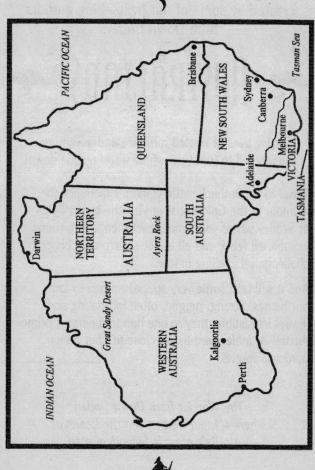

THE AUSTRALIANS

TAMING A HUSBAND
Elizabeth Duke

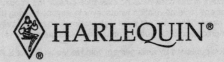

TORONTO • NEW YORK • LONDON
AMSTERDAM • PARIS • SYDNEY • HAMBURG
STOCKHOLM • ATHENS • TOKYO • MILAN • MADRID
PRAGUE • WARSAW • BUDAPEST • AUCKLAND

ISBN 0-373-82583-8

TAMING A HUSBAND

First North American Publication 1999.

Copyright © 1997 by Elizabeth Duke.

This edition published by arrangement with Harlequin Books S.A.

® and TM are trademarks of the publisher. Trademarks indicated with
® are registered in the United States Patent and Trademark Office, the
Canadian Trade Marks Office and in other countries.

Printed in U.S.A.

Elizabeth Duke was born in Adelaide, South Australia, but has lived in Melbourne all her married life. She trained as a librarian and has worked in many different types of libraries, but she was always secretly writing. Her first published book was a children's novel, after which she successfully tried her hand at romance writing. She has since given up her work as a librarian to write romance full-time. When she isn't writing or reading, she loves to travel with her husband, John, either within Australia or overseas, gathering inspiration and background material for future romances. She and John have a married son and daughter, who now have children of their own.

CHAPTER ONE

LEXIE placed a single white rose on her husband's coffin, her pale, delicately boned face a mask of dark-eyed composure. She felt numb, devoid of all feeling, uncomfortably aware of the waves of sympathy from Dominic's family and friends.

She wondered how long their sympathy would last if they knew she had been planning to leave Dominic, and that the overriding emotion she'd felt since the initial shock of his sudden death had been a numbing sense of release from the tension and emotional turmoil of the past months.

The simple ceremony was soon over. Faces blurred as one by one the mourners approached her to offer their condolences. Lexie accepted their hugs and handshakes, mouthing her thanks, their kindness bringing a pensive smile to her lips. It was going to be hard to leave these warm-hearted people, hard to leave Baulkham Hills and the only real security and warmth she'd ever known.

Everyone had been so kind to her, especially Bonnie and Cliff, who'd taken her in as a lost fourteen-year-old and had been like a mother and father to her long before she'd married their son. They'd made her feel as if she belonged to their family, that for the first time in her life she was genuinely loved and wanted. Their love had been unconditional and all-enveloping, expecting nothing in return.

But she had to go. She couldn't go on living here in Baulkham Hills, in their son's house, so close to *them*, his

parents. She couldn't go on living a lie—a lie that even
their son had grown uneasy with, to the point of paranoia.
It wouldn't be fair to Bonnie and Cliff.

'You must come home with us, dear.' Bonnie touched
her arm. 'We've asked a few people back for afternoon
tea.'

Lexie sucked in her lip. 'Bonnie, would you mind...?'
She avoided her mother-in-law's eye. 'I—I really don't
feel up to it. Everyone—' she gulped '—is being so kind.'
Too kind, she thought. I don't deserve it. I feel such a
fraud. 'And I'm anxious to get back to Sam.'

'Mary's with him, isn't she?' Bonnie's eyes softened at
the mention of the child she'd always believed to be her
grandson. 'She'll take good care of him, dear, until you
get home. She's such a capable person. So good with him.'

'It's been wonderful of you to spare her so often,
Bonnie. She's been such a help, both around the house and
with Sam.' Lexie hid a sigh. Life was going to be difficult
when she moved away and tried to earn a living on her
own. There would be no Mary to pop in to help with Sam,
or to give a hand around the house. No Bonnie to work in
partnership with, or to ask for advice. To say nothing of
losing the comforts and advantages she'd enjoyed as a
member of the Thorn family. But she would manage. She
had to. For Sam's sake.

Bonnie squeezed her arm. 'Mary loves looking after little Sam. As we all do. He's such an adorable child. So
sweet and well-behaved. Almost too well-behaved.' Her
normally lively grey eyes misted. 'He's so like Dominic
at the same age. He was quiet and placid too. Maybe not
as shy and timid as little Sam has been lately, but still so
like him. Oh, not in looks so much—he looks like you,
Lexie, especially with those big dark eyes of his and that
beautiful black hair. But there's no mistaking he's a Thorn.

There's something… It's hard to put a finger on it.' A wistful smile curved her lips. 'We've lost our son, but we have the consolation of knowing that he'll live on in Sam.'

Lexie's face showed pain for the first time. She bowed her head, letting her glossy black hair slide over her pale cheeks. Painfully difficult as it was going to be, she would have to tell Bonnie and Cliff the truth about Sam—without naming any names, of course—before she left. Even if they despised her for it, and never wanted to see her or Sam again. She couldn't go on living a lie, being a cherished member of their family, accepting their love, their generosity, their…trust. Not now that Dominic had gone. To keep up the deception would be using Bonnie and Cliff…accepting their kindness under false pretenses.

'Bonnie, you've been so good to me, you and Cliff,' she said impulsively. 'Taking me into your home when…when nobody else wanted me. Treating me like a daughter.'

'You *are* our daughter now, Lexie, dear…in every sense of the word,' Bonnie said, her eyes warm, glistening in the wintry sunlight. 'We were so happy when Dominic told us you were getting married. I admit it came as a shock. A pleasant shock,' she amended hastily. 'We'd always thought of you and Dominic as more…well, as more a loving brother and sister. Though, looking back, I should have guessed. Dominic adored you from the moment you came into our home. But for years you only had eyes for—' She caught back the rest, her smooth round cheeks flushing. 'Sorry, dear. I know you don't like being reminded of Jake. But he *is* my nephew. And, Lexie, dear, as a matter of fact he's going to be—'

'Sorry I'm late, Bonnie, my love.'

Lexie thought she was going to faint. Even without turning her head she knew who it was. That soft, deep voice was engraved on her soul.

Jake Thorn! The man who had loved her and walked away. The man who had broken her heart and shattered her dreams. The last man on earth that a homeless, motherless waif like Lexie Brown, who'd always craved a stable, secure home and a family of her own, should ever have fallen head over heels in love with.

How could he be here? He was somewhere in darkest Africa, half a world away!

'Jake, dear, you made it!' Bonnie threw out her plump arms and gathered Jake to her ample bosom, giving Lexie a merciful moment to draw breath. 'We weren't sure your plane would get you back home in time.'

'It almost didn't.' Jake lowered his voice to offer his condolences. 'Bonnie, my dear…what can I say? I know how close you always were to Dominic, you and Cliff.'

No mention of me, Lexie noted tautly. He didn't even appear to have noticed her.

Or had he?

She saw a shadow flit across Bonnie's round face. 'Not as close as we thought.' The bleak words leapt out, as if Bonnie couldn't hold them back. 'He'd denied there was anything wrong, but—'

She sighed as she explained, 'He'd changed, Jake. He'd become so withdrawn and morose. And touchy. He'd flare up over the slightest thing. It was so unlike him. He had no health problems. The—the post-mortem revealed that. Even poor Lexie couldn't explain why he was so—so moody and hard to get on with. I'm sure he would never—' her voice cracked '—would never have lost his footing on those iron stairs at the plant if his mind had been on what he was doing and not clouded with—with—'

She shook her head helplessly. 'I—I still can't believe it. That he's gone. Just one careless step. I just can't believe it.'

'No,' Jake said softly. 'That makes two of us.'

Much as she wanted to melt away and disappear, Lexie found that she couldn't move. Her dark eyes were drawn to Jake's strong profile, and she felt painful memories stirring at the sight of him, aware of a tightness growing in her chest, a breathlessness catching in her throat.

Jake, towering over Bonnie as he'd always towered over everybody, looked tougher, more deeply tanned, more ruggedly good-looking than ever, despite his broken nose, a legacy of his Amazon trip five years ago. She couldn't see his eyes from where she stood, but his brown hair was as thick and unruly as she'd last seen it three years ago, curling over his ears and round the collar of his grey shirt and casual jacket. No tie…not Jake…not even for a funeral. He looked rough and tough and untamed.

And dangerous. As dangerous as he'd always been. Dangerous to her emotions, to her peace of mind. To the whole fabric of her existence.

She had thought that she was over him. But now… seeing him again…this time with no Dominic to stand between them…

No! she thought explosively, rejecting the heart-stopping hope that had flared momentarily. You've been down that path before, you fool. You know where it leads. No point torturing yourself with futile, romantic dreams. Dreams turn into nightmares when Jake's around. The Jake Thorns of this world never change. You of all people should know that by now.

Besides, whatever had been between them once had long since crumbled to ashes. Bitter ashes. On both sides. Since Jake had come back from the Amazon three years ago and found that she'd married Dominic in his absence, they'd avoided each other, hated each other. She hated him for walking out on her and leaving her with no hope for a future together, no words of love to hold on to, for ruining her life and destroying her dreams. He hated her for turning so readily to Dominic the moment his back was turned…and for putting security and respectability ahead of the fulfilling, stimulating career she'd always been so adamant she wanted. The career she'd sworn she wanted to share with *him*.

How could they ever go back to the way it had once been? It was far too late.

Bonnie was still clutching Jake's arm. 'It happened so quickly, Jake,' she whispered, shaking her head in disbelief. 'There was nothing anyone could do. The—the fall broke his neck. He was killed instantly.' Tears spread across her eyes. 'Just one moment of carelessness. It was so unlike Dominic. He was always so careful. In everything he did.'

'Well, at least he didn't suffer.' Jake's voice was unusually gentle, gentler than Lexie had ever heard it. Certainly a lot gentler than the last time she'd heard it, when he'd found her married to Dominic. Married, with a fourteen-month-old child.

'You're right. Carelessness—reckless behaviour—were never Dominic's style. More mine,' he added with a sardonic twist of his lip. 'Does Cliff have any idea why he'd changed so much?'

'No.' Bonnie shook her head, blinking away tears. 'But Dominic had become so listless and apathetic at work that Cliff was worried he might be losing interest in the business and getting ready to toss it in…the way you did, Jake, when your father died and you sold his share of the business. But that was different,' she hastened to add, with no condemnation in her voice. 'We all knew you had other ambitions. But Dominic…' She gulped before going on.

'He was always so keen to be involved in the family

business, so keen to keep it going, and see it flourish. For his son, he told us the day little Sam was born.' She gave a baffled sigh. 'It wasn't as if the business hadn't been doing well. It's more prosperous than it's ever been. So why should he have lost interest? No…' Her eyes clouded. 'It had to be something else.'

'The responsibilities of marriage, perhaps?' Jake drawled, and Lexie stiffened, her lips tightening at the lazy cynicism in his voice. What, she wanted to snarl at him, would you know about the responsibilities of marriage, Jake Thorn?

Bonnie rejected the suggestion with a fierce shake of her head. 'Dominic loved being married. He had everything he'd ever wanted. A beautiful, supportive wife, a fine, healthy son, a lovely home, a loving family living close by, financial security.' Her eyes darkened in pain. 'So what could have made him change so much? *You* remember how he used to be, Jake? He was always so easygoing and contented. So steady and reliable. So…settled.'

'Unlike his wayward cousin,' Jake said dryly, and Lexie's dark eyes sharpened. Had he just said that to take Bonnie's mind off Dominic? It didn't sound like something he would normally admit.

'Oh, Jake, I didn't mean—' Bonnie broke off, looking flustered. 'That wasn't a shot at you, dear. You might be something of an—an adventurer, but you're also one of Australia's—the *world's*—top photo-journalists. No one could ever call you *wayward*, dear…' She smiled mistily up at him. 'Even if you do love to dice with danger— death too, at times. I think you risk your life for the sheer love of it.'

For the sheer *hell* of it, Lexie thought darkly. Jake didn't know the meaning of the word 'love'.

Jake gave a wry smile and drew back, straightening,

turning his head at last. 'Lexie.' He eased himself out of Bonnie's grasp and held out his hand.

Lexie pretended not to see it, willing herself to look up into his face. Somehow, though it took a supreme effort, she met his gaze without so much as a flicker. It was painfully difficult to maintain her steady gaze. His piercing blue eyes—even bluer than she remembered them— seemed to swallow her whole. She couldn't read what was in the glinting depths. She didn't even try. Too many flickering emotions lay there. None of them, she imagined, at all sympathetic!

'So…the prodigal returns.' She used her coolest, calmest tone, careful to keep all expression from her voice. Hoping he wouldn't realise how much she was trembling. Or try to take her hand, and feel its clamminess. To make sure he didn't she folded her arms, curling her hands underneath.

'Oh, Jake, dear, forgive me!' Bonnie thrust her plump face between them. 'I've been so selfish and thoughtless, crying on your shoulder all this time while Lexie here is being so brave and strong. I must go and find Cliff, and then we'll be off. Jake—' She hesitated, then seemed to make up her mind. 'Would you be a dear and see Lexie home? She doesn't feel up to coming back to our place…facing people. And she's anxious to get back to Sam. We'll catch up with you both later. You must come for a meal. Tonight, if you feel up to it.'

Lexie nodded vaguely, and drew in a deep breath, weighing up whether to change her mind and go back to Bonnie's place after all. Weighing up which would be worse. Going home with Jake, being alone with him, even if she managed to get rid of him the moment he dropped her there…or facing the sympathy of Dominic's friends and relatives and having to endure their talk about

Dominic, having to pretend that she was broken-hearted and merited their sympathy.

'I'd really rather be alone,' she said at length. 'I have my own car...' She certainly didn't want to risk Jake forcing—or coaxing—his way into her home, and seeing Sam, who was now three years older than the sleeping baby he'd briefly glimpsed back then. What if he saw the signs and tell-tale mannerisms that Dominic had convinced himself were there, that possibly *were* there? She wasn't ready to face that yet. If ever. She needed time to think!

How long did Jake intend to stay in Australia?

'You're not driving yourself home,' Jake said firmly. 'Don't worry, Bonnie.' His gaze flicked briefly to his aunt, who was still waiting, her teeth tugging at her lip. 'I'll see her safely home. And catch up with Cliff later.'

'Thanks, Jake.' Bonnie's grey eyes appealed to Lexie as she backed away. Be kind to him, they seemed to be pleading with her.

Lexie smiled wanly.

Jake was already steering her away. She didn't protest, not wanting to make a scene and have Bonnie or any of the others wondering why she didn't want Dominic's cousin to see her home. Besides, she'd already changed her mind about not wanting to be alone with Jake. She *needed* to be alone with him, she realised. For a short time, at least. If only to find out precisely why he'd come back. He'd never been close to Dominic, so why would he rush all the way back from Africa, presumably in the midst of one of his crucial assignments, to attend his cousin's funeral?

Simply for Bonnie's sake? And Cliff's? Hardly for hers!

'Got your keys?' he asked as they reached her late-model Holden station wagon.

'I'll drive,' she said, not wanting him to think he could

start taking over her life now that he was back. Now that Dominic was no longer around. No longer there between them. He would find that she was a lot older and wiser and tougher—and far more self-reliant—than the immature, clinging, starry-eyed creature he'd walked out on five years ago. If he had any wild thoughts about picking up where he'd left off—of bedding her and waltzing off again, to vanish into the wilds of wherever his work and his love of adventure took him next—he could forget it.

That was the last thing she wanted. A casual, fly-by-night love affair with Jake. A fly-by-night lover. A fly-by-night father for Sam. Sam deserved more...*needed* more. He needed all the love and security and happiness she could give him. And she *would*. Sam was the one she must think of now.

'You're not driving.' Jake's hand closed over hers. 'You're shaking like a leaf. Is it grief, Lexie?' He lifted a dark eyebrow. 'Or is it...me?'

'You!' She almost spat the word at him. 'You think the minute you come back—' She snapped off the rest, with a sharp toss of her head that made her flowing black hair shimmer in the afternoon sunlight. She began again, pricklingly conscious of his hand curled warmly over her own. 'You lost the power to affect me long ago, Jake Thorn.' She laced the brave words with scorn. But the taunt sounded as hollow to her own ears as it was in reality.

'That's too bad.' He blew out his breath, his fingers momentarily tightening their grip on hers. 'Sorry, Lexie...that was uncalled for.' He didn't *sound* sorry, didn't look it. Not a bit. 'I guess now is hardly the time—'

'Or any other time!' she bit back, self-preservation prompting the withering retort. Whatever she still felt for Jake, whatever lingering effect he still had on her, she'd be a fool to show it, to give in to it, let alone start resurrecting old hopes, fanciful dreams.

Never again would she fall into the trap of believing that she had the power to hold him, to change him…that she meant more to him than his blazing ambition, his need for challenge and adventure and death-defying danger. Nothing would change Jake Thorn but Jake himself. It would be disastrous to try. She'd only end up being hurt again. Being left alone again. Jake was a past master at loving and leaving. Never again would she let herself be that vulnerable to him. Or to anyone.

Jake plucked the keys from her hand. 'Let me drive, Lexie.' It was a request this time, not a demand. 'How come you have your car here anyway? Surely you came in one of the official limos?'

'I did.' She shrugged. 'Someone was kind enough to drive my car here for me.'

'To ensure an easy escape route?' Again, that mocking lift of his brow.

The sight of it hardened her heart. He had never believed that she'd married Dominic for love. Whether he was right or not was beside the point. He had no right to come back and taunt her about it. Today of all days.

'If anyone knows about easy escape routes, it's you, Jake, not me!' she flung back. The second the hot words left her lips she could have bitten out her tongue. Reminding Jake of the past would only confirm what he suspected already. That she still wasn't over him. That she'd married Dominic on the rebound, out of hurt, or spite, or childish anger.

If only it were that simple.

'Drive, then, if you insist!' She pulled open the passenger door and climbed in, staring stonily ahead as Jake stepped around to the driver's side and slid in beside her.

As the car moved off, she silently berated herself for bringing up the past. What was the point? She had no wish to be reminded of youthful, romantic dreams. Of dreams shattered. Jake would hardly want to be reminded either.

'Why did you come back?' The blunt question leapt out. 'You never cared about Dominic.'

For a second she thought he wasn't going to answer. But after a pause he did, his lip twisting as he conceded, 'We were never bosom buddies...granted. Especially in these past three years.' His face darkened. 'I didn't come back,' he told her levelly, 'to cry crocodile tears over Dominic.'

She drew in a quick, tremulous breath. 'Then why—?' She broke off abruptly, her mouth feeling suddenly like sandpaper. She wished she hadn't asked. Damn it, what was she expecting to hear? Protestations of undying love, now that Dominic was out of the picture? Some hope! Even if Jake dropped to his knees and *swore* undying love, what would it be worth, without commitment? Jake didn't believe in commitment, in putting down roots. She'd be mad not to keep that in mind.

'Why did I come back for my cousin's funeral?' A brief smile touched his lips as he echoed her question. Almost as if he'd sensed her inner turmoil, and was relishing it. He still wasn't looking at her, his eyes steady on the road in front. Was he afraid to, in case he saw in her eyes what he suspected might be there? Jake would run a mile, she didn't doubt, if he thought she still wanted him, still wanted to *tie him down*.

Unless... She gulped hard as another possibility occurred to her. Unless he was simply respecting her period of mourning. Holding back...for the time being. Would Jake Thorn have the sensitivity to wait, if he wanted her? But wanted her for *what*? And for how long?

CHAPTER TWO

'I THOUGHT the least I could do was come back and pay my respects to my aunt and uncle.' Jake's tone was silky. 'And...' his taunting gaze flicked round '...to the grieving widow. *Are* you grieving, Lexie? You look very calm and in control to me. Not even a tear.'

She swallowed again, her body tensing. What else did he see? 'I'm not the giddy, emotional girl you used to know, Jake,' she retorted. 'I don't wear my heart on my sleeve the way I once did. Whatever I feel is...' She faltered. 'I keep to myself.'

'It's not a good idea to bottle things up, Lexie. If you need—'

'*Need?*' she cut in scathingly, her nerves stretched to breaking point. 'What would you know about my needs, Jake Thorn? You've never cared about me or my needs before!' Even as the stinging words tumbled out, she knew she was being unfair. As he was quick to point out.

'No? Think back, Lexie.' His mouth curved in a sardonic half-smile. 'Why don't we go right back...to when we first met? Who was around that night when you were cowering under the Sydney Harbour Bridge—a tearful, frightened, but very determined fourteen-year-old runaway, hiding from your father and stepmother? Who rescued you and took you in? Not Dominic. *Me.*'

She sniffed, dismissing the trauma of that long-ago winter with a toss of her head. 'Dominic was only a teenager then. A schoolboy. You were twenty-four...ten years older than me. You were like a—a caring older brother.'

His brow shot up. 'There was never anything brotherly between you and me, Lexie. Dominic was always the one you looked on as a brother. Or you did back then.' Cynicism hardened his voice.

Lexie held a sigh. No, she thought. I never looked on you as a big brother, Jake. You were my knight in shining armour. My hero. I'd never come across anyone like you. You were like one of those tough, rough-diamond, rugged-faced heroes women swoon over in adventure movies. The kind who crash through jungles and gallop across deserts. Hard-bitten, tough as nails on the outside, but with a heart as big as a house when a damsel's in distress.

Or a tearful, homeless waif.

She lapsed into silence, giving in for a moment to bittersweet memories. She'd had an enormous crush on Jake from the moment she'd first glimpsed him through the blur of her tears on that cold, desolate night in the lonely back streets of Sydney. She recalled how she'd squeezed her eyes shut to clear them, and then opened them again, her gaze fluttering up the tanned column of the stranger's throat, over his strong jawline to firm, sensual lips and a nose that was straight and unbroken then. Only to be dazzled a second later by a pair of the most incredibly blue eyes.

She sighed again, trembling at the memory of that first stunning impression of him. The deeply bronzed face, showing his concern. The hefty shoulders and muscular arms, showing his strength. The camera bag slung over his shoulder, as it always was in those days. She'd felt no fear, strangely.

'Is that a sigh for Dominic, Lexie?' Jake's mocking question shattered the image in her mind.

'I don't want to talk about Dominic!' Her tone was fractious. 'And I don't want to talk about my father either.'

Her lip curled. 'He *wasn't* my father, as you well know. I never had a father. Or a mother either. Nobody even knew who my real mother was. A teenage drug addict most likely, whose only motherly act was to leave me on a hospital doorstep rather than tossing me out with the garbage!'

Suddenly, without her wanting it to, the long-buried pain spilt out in a flood of bitter memories. 'I only ever had foster parents after foster parents, until I was adopted at the age of seven by a couple in their forties who were considered too old to adopt a baby. My new mother, well-meaning as she was, was never fit or strong and died of cancer five years later. Just two years after that my weak, ineffectual "father" married again—married a real witch of a woman who hated me from the start. She couldn't wait to get rid of me. And she did!'

'She was jealous of you, Lexie,' Jake said mildly. 'I realised that when I went to see them. The way she accused you of flashing your dark eyes and tossing your black hair to "take people in". The way she was so derogatory about your "way with words", as she called it. She resented both your looks and the fact that you were doing so brilliantly at school, especially in English. It was pure spite on her part—fuelled by her jealousy—that made her talk your father into selling up and moving north to Queensland, leaving you behind.'

'Intending to force me to board with a family she knew I couldn't stand,' Lexie muttered with a scowl. 'A family she knew would take me out of school and put me to work in their crummy fish shop. She tried to tell me she was doing me a favour, setting up a job for me. Never mind about school. What did a miserable creature like me need with an education? Can you blame me for running away?'

'You know I never blamed you for that, Lexie.'

For a lot of other things, Lexie thought, but not that.

'You were the answer to their prayers, Jake, taking me off their hands,' she told him wryly. 'They couldn't wait to wash their hands of me.' As people had been washing their hands of her, or abandoning her for one reason or another, her entire life.

'Look...I know your early life was tough on you, Lexie,' Jake commiserated, glancing round at her. 'But you were happy when my aunt and uncle took you in, weren't you?'

She nodded, her thick lashes fluttering down over her pale cheeks. Dominic's parents had been wonderful to her, bringing her up as if she'd been their own daughter. Giving her love, giving her the best education, even giving her their beloved only son. But for how much longer would she have their support, their love? Once they found out that she'd been lying to them about Sam being Dominic's son—and their grandson—they would want to abandon her too...if she didn't walk away from them first and save them the trouble. And spare them any additional pain and distress.

She jumped as she felt Jake touch her arm. 'I'll need a bed for the night,' he murmured. 'I sold my family home three years ago, remember, and I haven't been back since. You're not going to make me go to a motel, are you?' The mocking thread was back in his voice.

Her eyes leapt to his, her heart giving a frantic flutter. 'Won't you be staying with Bonnie and Cliff?'

'Not with all those other relatives around. They'll have their hands full.'

She bit her lip. 'I...I don't think—'

'If you're thinking of the proprieties, Lexie, now that you're a single woman again—'

'Widow,' she corrected him sharply.

'Whatever. Why don't you ask Mary to stay the night,

if you feel in need of a chaperon?' he drawled, his tone as sardonic as the faint smile on his lips.

Trust him to remember Mary, Bonnie's long-time housekeeper. Normally Mary lived in at Bonnie's place, but since Dominic's death Bonnie had insisted that Mary stay with Lexie, for as long as she needed her. Mary was at home caring for Sam now. Only she was going to be out this evening, Lexie remembered. She was going to her niece's wedding, and intended to stay the night at her sister's.

She lifted her chin. 'I hardly think—'

'And there's your son.'

Lexie's heart stopped. A lump settled in her throat. It was a moment before she could force any words out. 'I— I'd really rather be alone right now,' she heard herself blurt out. It was too soon! Too soon for him to see Sam. She wasn't prepared for it yet. 'I—I don't think I could cope with a—a house guest.'

'I'm hardly a house guest, Lexie. I'm family, remember.'

'You're not *my* family,' she said heatedly. 'We're not related in any way!'

'By marriage we are.' How infuriatingly calm he was, his keen blue eyes coolly impassive, giving no clue to whatever thoughts were going on behind them. 'We're cousins by marriage, Lexie. And I also happen to be a *blood* relative of your son—his second cousin. I'm the closest thing to an uncle that young Sam will ever have.' He paused, slanting a look at her. 'I'd like to get to know him, Lexie.'

She felt a flare of panic, a strangling sensation in her throat. No...it was too soon. What if he—?

Clenching her hands in her lap, she sucked in a fractured breath, then let it out in a tremulous sigh. Damn it...why

not? Why bother to keep them apart? If Jake saw something of himself in Sam, wouldn't he simply put it down
to a family likeness? Cousins often did look alike. Didn't
she *want* Jake to get to know Sam, now that Dominic had
gone from their lives? Even though Jake wasn't aware yet
that Sam was his son, it was important—only fair and
right—that they meet and get to know each other. And by
letting Jake stay at her house...

'All right.' She shrugged, feigning nonchalance. 'I'd
like Sam to get to know his...his uncle Jake. Are
you...back home for long?' She held her breath, willing
him—foolishly—to say that he'd come back for good, to
announce that his endless adventuring, his wanderlust, his
days of living on the edge in the most perilous corners of
the world were behind him.

'Only for a few days, unfortunately. I'm in the midst of
an assignment...a series of articles.' His shoulders lifted
and fell. 'The break will do me good. I haven't had one
in quite a while.'

He was only back in Australia for a few *days*? Some
break! Lexie's heart plunged, her last dim hope dying.

'You're...going back to Africa?' she asked stupidly,
forcing the words out.

He nodded. 'There's no immediate urgency. I can stay
for a week or so...no problem.'

'How nice that you don't have to rush back,' she said,
barely bothering to hide her sarcasm. Damn it, what did
she expect? That Jake might have changed? That he might
have decided finally to settle down—for *good*? Jake Thorn
would never change, would never want to settle down to
a tame, domesticated life at home. The Jakes of this world
had no wish or need to put down roots, no need for a
family, for a normal home life, for close blood-ties...for
security.

All the things *she* needed, and had secretly always longed for—even more fiercely since Sam had come into her life. And she still did want those things, despite the mess she'd made of her life in the pursuit of that dream...despite her drastic mistake in believing that Dominic could provide the security and happiness she and her child needed...despite the gradual disillusionment that had followed her hasty decision to marry him five years ago.

She still had Sam. Her son. Her own flesh and blood. Her *sole* blood relative in the whole wide world. Nobody could take Sam away from her. With or without Jake Thorn in her life, she was going to make sure that her child grew up with the love and the security that she herself had never had.

Yes... From now on, she intended to take control of her life. If she couldn't have Jake permanently in her life—a foolish pipedream if ever there was one, which their bitter differences and old grievances made doubly futile—she would do it alone. As she'd been planning to do before Dominic's fatal accident.

'You're looking wistful, Lexie...showing a bit of feeling for the first time.' Jake's soft voice, faintly laced with irony, brought her back from her pensive reverie. 'What are you thinking about? Dominic? Or...how you're going to get rid of *me*?'

Flushing, she snapped back to life, feeling ashamed that she had indeed been thinking of him rather than Dominic. She answered with a touch of scorn, deliberately misunderstanding him. 'Why would I want to get rid of you? You have every right to be here. You're a Thorn. A part of the Thorn family.' More a part than she was...now, she acknowledged.

'How kind of you to say so,' Jake responded dryly. 'Most people see me as the black sheep of the family. The one who threw away his inheritance—and his girl—to wander the world taking useless photographs.'

She tensed, but the face she turned to him was an impassive mask. No way would she give him the satisfaction of reacting to the words 'and his girl'. He was implying that they'd had some kind of commitment. That he'd loved her. Jake had never loved her...not the way she'd yearned for him to love her. She had wanted him to give her his heart and his soul, but he had only ever given her his body. It was all he'd been prepared to give. All he would ever be prepared to give. And even that had been given in the heat of passion, not with any thought of the consequences. Or the future.

'You know your photographs are not useless, Jake,' she said in a voice as steady as she could manage. 'They're in demand all over the world.' Inside, she felt anything *but* steady. She felt as if she was disintegrating, bits of her chipping off into myriads of tiny pieces. Didn't he realise what he was doing to her, coming back now, when she was at her most vulnerable? She could feel her heart crying out from deep inside her, I'm free at last, but what good is it going to do me? He's only back home for a few days!

'You've been following my career, Lexie?' Jake asked, his eyes half-narrowed, hooded, hiding his own feelings as carefully as she was hiding hers.

'As a member of the Thorn family, naturally I've been interested in your...successes. Bonnie and Cliff have kept us informed...from time to time.' She glanced out the window. 'It's the last house on the left...in case you've forgotten.'

'I haven't forgotten.'

She swallowed, keeping her face averted until Jake swung the station wagon through the front gates of her federation-style home. She and Dominic had restored the house together…in the days when he was still enthusiastic about his marriage, and about making a beautiful home for her and Sam. She would have to sell it now, of course. Whatever she made from the sale she would need to buy another house. A smaller house on a smaller plot of land, closer to the city. Even so, houses near the city, even modest ones, were expensive. There wasn't likely to be anything left over.

It was just as well she'd been putting aside a bit of money lately—expecting to need it when she left home with Sam. She could hardly have expected anything from Dominic. It gave her a twinge of guilt to think that, because of a stroke of fate, Dominic's house, which was in both their names, would now be hers.

Anything else… She shook her head. Even if Dominic had left her his shares in the family business, which was doubtful, it would be wrong to accept them, wrong even to sell them back to his family. She would give them to Bonnie and Cliff. They belonged to the Thorns. They would not pass on to Sam one day in the future…not now.

She was out of the car before Jake could step around to open the door for her.

'Where's your luggage?' she asked without enthusiasm. Maybe, if he considered again, he would change his mind about staying the night at her house. He must have realised by now how uncomfortable it would be for them both, being under the same roof.

He gave her a look that was almost sheepish. 'I took the liberty of asking my taxi-driver to deliver my bag to your place after he'd dropped me off at the funeral. I'd come straight from the airport, you see, and was running late.'

'You… What a cheek!' Angry red spots leapt to her cheeks. 'You're saying you *knew* I'd let you stay?' Even as she spluttered her protest, she was aware of a treacherous twinge of relief, which only inflamed her further. 'How did you know there'd be someone at home to take your bag?'

'I didn't. I paid the fellow in advance—generously— and told him to leave it on your front porch if nobody was at home.'

'With your precious camera equipment inside?' She looked at him in astonishment. 'Weren't you worried that someone might come along and pinch it? Or that the taxi- driver himself might run off with it?'

'There's no photographic equipment in my bag…only a few clothes. I left my camera and the rest of my stuff back in Africa.'

'Oh, yes…Africa,' Her mouth twisted. 'You're going straight back, you said.'

'Not *straight* back,' he reminded her in a soft drawl. 'I have about a week. Long enough to help you…in whatever way I can.'

Her eyes snapped to his, dark with rejection, even as something deep down inside her was urging her to grasp his offer with both hands. 'I don't need your help, Jake Thorn,' she said in a stifled voice. 'I'm quite capable of managing my own life, thanks!'

'Are you, Lexie?' His tone was faintly derisive now. 'You've never been on your own before. You went straight from your cosy bed at Bonnie and Cilff's, if I recall, to the bed you shared with Dominic—which presumably you kept on sharing up until his death last week.'

She clenched her hands into white-knuckled fists, her cheeks flaming, her small white teeth gritted in suppressed fury. It took all her effort not to lash out at him for walking out of her life five years ago, for not being there when she'd needed him the most, for causing her to turn to Dominic because *he'd* been offering what she'd known Jake never would.

She swept past him up the front steps, fervently hoping in that moment that he would decide to turn around and walk out of her life again, before he could cause her any more heartache.

But a weak, traitorous part of her was willing him to stay, and when she heard his footsteps behind her she swallowed hard and let her clenched hands relax.

But only for a moment. She tensed again as the front door swung open and Mary appeared, her matronly figure masked by a floral apron. Lexie's gaze flicked anxiously past her, seeking Sam's smooth, dark mop of hair, or his big black eyes peeking round Mary's skirt.

'Sam's taking a nap,' Mary said, and Lexie slowly released her breath. 'How did it go, love? Nice service, was it?' Mary's soft brown eyes were warmly sympathetic. Big-boned and fiftyish, she looked as calm and unflappable as always. No demanding pre-school child, no household chore, no family crisis ever fazed Mary. No one would ever have guessed that she had a family wedding to go to later in the day.

'Mr Thorn!' Mary's eyes lit up as Jake's broad-shouldered frame filled the doorway behind Lexie.

'Hullo, Mary.' Jake stepped into the carpeted hall. 'Glad to see the Thorn family haven't driven you away just yet.'

'Oh, Mr Thorn!' Mary giggled—something Lexie hadn't heard, she realised, for some time. There had been little spontaneous laughter in the Thorn household in recent months.

Mary caught the shadow that crossed her face and sobered instantly. 'Oh, love, I'm sorry,' she said swiftly. 'This is no time for frivolity.'

'Don't be silly, Mary.' Lexie touched her arm as she

brushed past her. 'Dominic wouldn't want us to be miserable.'

Wouldn't he? a small voice mocked. He'd done his best to make their lives as miserable as his own these past months...as Mary must have noticed on the occasions she'd been here. Anyone at close quarters would have sensed the strained atmosphere, and noticed the change in Dominic...to say nothing of the subtle, disturbing change in Sam from a happy, contented toddler to the timid, withdrawn little boy he was today.

'I knew you were back home, Mr Thorn.' Mary's smile flashed again. 'Your taxi-driver dropped your suitcase off earlier.' She glanced uncertainly at Lexie. 'The spare room's made up...if it's needed.'

'Thank you, Mary. Bonnie and Cliff have other relatives in town at present, so Mr Thorn will be staying here overnight,' Lexie said impassively. Maybe Jake would take the hint and only stay for one night. She looked appealingly at Mary. 'You'll be back after your niece's wedding, won't you, Mary, to stay for a few more days?' she asked anxiously, in case Jake did decide to stay on for more than one night. 'Bonnie says she can manage without you for the rest of the week, since we've cancelled all our functions and dinners for the time being.'

'You're still helping Bonnie with her catering business?' Jake's soft voice intervened.

Lexie raised her chin a notch. 'Bonnie and I have been *partners* for some time,' she corrected him. 'In fact—' now was as good a chance as any to let them know what she was thinking of doing '—I'm planning to use my cooking expertise when Sam and I leave here and move closer to the city.'

'You're thinking of selling up and leaving Baulkham Hills?'

She heard the sharp surprise—or was it censure?—in Jake's voice. Uncomfortably aware of his glinting blue eyes probing hers, she avoided them steadfastly, turning to Mary instead.

'Oh, love, you're not!' Mary cried, her usually calm face showing her shock.

'You're not to say anything!' Lexie said sharply. Not that Mary would. She was the soul of discretion. But Jake might. 'I haven't told Bonnie yet. I've only just decided. I…' She hesitated. 'I want to make a completely fresh start.' No need to admit to them that she'd been planning to leave even before Dominic's death. 'I'd like to tell her myself,' she said firmly.

Mary bit her lip. 'Yes, of course…'

'Would you mind making a pot of tea, Mary?' Lexie said quickly, before either of them could ask any more questions. 'I'm sure Jake could do with a cup. He's just flown in from Africa. And then you must go and get ready for your niece's wedding.' She swung round, heading for the bedrooms.

'I'll show you to your room, Jake, and you can clean up while Mary's making the tea. There's a bathroom opposite your room. You'll have it to yourself,' she informed him crisply, not wanting him to get any ideas about sharing one. About sharing anything.

CHAPTER THREE

LEXIE felt her hand trembling as she raised her cup and took a long sip of her tea. Things might have been a bit easier if Mary had stayed with them, but she'd vanished to her room—or retired discreetly?—to get ready for her niece's wedding.

I should have gone back to Bonnie's place after all, she mused edgily. Being among Dominic's friends and relatives would have been preferable to being here alone with Jake, where she had no escape from those piercing blue eyes. In a crowd, she could have avoided him. Here, she couldn't.

The air between them was thick, tense, throbbing with painful, bitter-sweet memories...unspoken resentments...niggling questions. And a breathless sexual tension.

It was Jake who finally broke the silence.

'You've grown more beautiful, Lexie. You would have made a stunning television reporter, you know, if you'd gone ahead with your career in journalism,' he said pointedly. 'With those extraordinary black eyes of yours and that exotic blue-black hair and milk-white skin...along with your husky, sexy voice, which has grown deeper, huskier over the years...you would have been a knockout on TV.'

'I never wanted to be on TV!' she flashed back with scorn, her heart twisting at his description of her. 'I wanted to *write*. Articles, features, stories...'

'Then why didn't you?'

'I had a home and a baby to look after!' she snapped. 'I couldn't spend my time going out chasing stories. Anyway, I didn't want to. I wanted to be with my child. It's what I always wanted, remember? To be a mother…and a wife.' *Your wife, Jake, only you didn't want to be tied down.* You were too obsessed with rushing off to the other side of the world and risking your neck, living your dangerous life to the full…without any encumbrances.

'You didn't have a home and a baby when I went off to the Amazon,' Jake reminded her with a curl of his lip. 'Before I left, you wanted to set the world ablaze with your articles and stories. Or was that just a ploy from the beginning, Lexie, to keep me on a string?'

His eyes seared hers. 'That's it, isn't it? Or you wouldn't have tossed it all in virtually overnight the moment Dominic came up with a better offer. Why don't you admit that you married him to hit back at me for not taking you with me to the Amazon? Or, more to the point, for not doing what you really wanted me to do—staying at home and being what *you* wanted me to be!'

'That's not—' Lexie began, and stopped, her heart shrivelling. How could she defend herself without…? 'Please, Jake…not now!' The plea burst from her, almost a wail.

'Sorry,' Jake said gruffly. 'You're right. Now's not the time. Besides, we went through all this three years ago.' He sank back in his chair with a sigh, studying her face with less fire in his eyes this time as he nibbled on one of Mary's sultana cakes.

'Your eyes,' he murmured after a pause, 'always were your most stunning feature, Lexie. But they're even more striking now. There's more depth, maturity, wisdom, deeper shades of emotion. Is that…pain I see there too, Lexie?' he probed, a softer note in his voice now.

Her grip tightened on the cup in her hand. 'I've just lost my husband!' she scraped out. 'What do you expect?'

'Is that what it is, Lexie?' His gaze pinned hers. 'I would have said that those shadows in your eyes, that bruised, haunted look, have been there for some time.'

She jerked in her chair. 'I—that's—'

'Were you happy with him, Lexie?'

She dragged in her breath, tugging her eyes away from his with an effort, fixing her gaze on her teacup. How could she answer that…truthfully? She couldn't. She had to go on pretending…if only for Bonnie's sake, and Cliff's.

Only for theirs?

'Please…' She shifted restlessly in her chair. 'I'd rather not talk about Dominic. Not…just now.' If she told him the truth about her marriage to Dominic, particularly over these past few months, Jake might guess other truths, truths she wasn't ready to deal with just yet.

'Well, then, tell me about your son, Lexie. I imagine he's changed somewhat since I saw him as a baby?' Some dark emotion stirred in the intense blue depths of his eyes, as if he was remembering, against his will, his traumatic homecoming three years ago. 'He'd be…what?…four by now?'

'Four and a bit.' She nodded, swallowing. Sam had been just over a year old the last time Jake had seen him…the *only* time he'd ever seen him. It had been one of the most harrowing times of her life, that day Jake had come back, without any warning, after nearly two years lost—lost to the outside world at least—in the torturous wilds of the Amazon. Two years, without a word.

'He's…fine,' she said carefully, wishing she could

sound more enthusiastic, wishing she could tell Jake that Sam was a happy, outgoing, carefree child—the way he'd once been.

'You sound a bit hesitant,' Jake said. 'You're worried about him?'

She sucked in a quick breath. She'd forgotten how perceptive Jake had always been. 'Well…' she paused, then gave a quick shrug. 'He's just lost his father. He's bound to be…affected by it.' To avoid Jake's eye, she twisted round to set her empty cup down on the small table beside her. Hopefully, Sam would begin to come out of his shell a bit more now, and gradually regain his confidence, his old sunny nature. Now that Dominic had gone.

'Children are resilient,' she said, settling back again. 'He'll be all right. He still has me. We're…very close.'

'And his grandparents.'

She inhaled slowly. 'Of course.' But for how much longer would he have them? Would Bonnie and Cliff *want* to see them any more, *want* to keep in touch, once they knew that Sam wasn't their grandson? Or would they choose to cut the ties between them completely? As people connected to her had been breaking ties with her from as far back as she could remember.

At least Sam will still have *me*, Lexie thought fiercely. He'll always have me.

'So…the boy's lost his father, and now you want to take him away from his grandparents as well.' There was sharp condemnation in Jake's voice. 'It works the other way too, you know, Lexie. Think of *them*…Bonnie and Cliff. They've lost their son—their only child—and now you want to take their only grandson away from them too. And their daughter. You *are* a daughter to them, Lexie. The daughter they never had.'

She looked down at the hands in her lap, her lips pursing. Bonnie had said the same thing…that she was like a daughter to them. But Jake didn't understand! She didn't *want* to leave them. But she had to! She couldn't go on letting them swamp her with love and kindness under false pretences; she couldn't go on lying to them, pretending that her child was their son's flesh and blood. She'd been planning to *leave* Dominic, for heaven's sake!

She sighed, twisting her hands together. On the other hand…Bonnie and Cliff had loved her as a daughter long before she'd married Dominic. And they'd loved Sam from the day she'd given birth to him. Maybe the thought of losing the two of them from their lives, on top of losing their son, would be even more devastating to them than learning the truth about Sam? Dominic's child or not, Sam was still the nearest thing to a grandson that they would ever have…

And Sam was, in actual fact, related to them by birth, even though she couldn't tell them that—at least, not until she'd confessed to Jake. Sam's father, Jake, was their nephew, the son of Cliff's older brother. Dominic's first cousin.

Her eyelashes fluttered upwards. 'I…I won't be taking Sam away from Bonnie and Cliff,' she whispered. 'I'm not moving to the country, or to another state .' She didn't add that she'd considered both options at one time, when Dominic was still alive. 'I'll still be here in Sydney, within easy reach.'

She breathed deeply, chewing on her lip. Would it be wicked of her to go on letting Bonnie and Cliff believe, for the time being, that Sam *was* their grandson, *was* Dominic's child? And let them go on seeing her, visiting her, whenever they wanted to? She would still have to move out of her home, of course, away from Baulkham Hills. She couldn't stay on in Dominic's house, or even here in his home town! But why make things harder, more painful, for Bonnie and Cliff by telling them the truth before she left?

Besides…if she confessed to them now that Sam wasn't Dominic's child—before she told Jake—they would surely guess whose child he was. How naive of her to imagine that they wouldn't! Who else had she been close to five years ago but Jake?

She gulped. Hard. No. She couldn't tell them. *Or* Jake. Not yet. Jake probably wouldn't believe her, anyway. He'd think she was lying to him, in the hope of trapping him into staying in Australia, into staying with *her*. She'd lied to him once before, he would point out—never mind that it was with the best of intentions—after they'd made love that one and only time.

She flushed now at the memory of that impulsive lie. Telling him she was on the pill! True, it had come in useful three years ago when Jake had stormed back into their lives. But Dominic had been alive then, and she'd *had* to stick to her lie to convince Jake that her baby son wasn't his.

But now Dominic had gone. And that foolish lie was going to rebound on her. Jake would accuse her of lying *again*—this time about Sam being his son. Even if she did manage to convince him, she might as well be putting a gun to his head. He would feel he *had* to stay in Australia, for his son's sake. He probably would stay too. He would do the right thing, the honourable thing. And after a while he'd feel trapped, stifled, resentful. He'd grow bitter and frustrated. And she knew what bitterness and frustration could do to a man.

She leaned back in her chair and closed her eyes.

'I really don't feel up to talking any more right now,' she said wearily. 'Why don't you go to your room, Jake, and take a nap? You must be feeling jet-lagged after flying all that way. I'll have to bath Sam shortly. He should be awake any minute. He doesn't normally sleep this long during the day, if at all.' Since Dominic's death, four days ago, Sam had resumed his daytime naps...as if he'd been storing up the need in the past uneasy months. As if he was finally allowing himself to relax.

Jake's voice came back, vibrating through her. 'This chair's very comfy...I'm perfectly happy here. I'm used to dozing off in far less cosy places than this.'

As silence fell between them, Lexie let her mind drift back to the blissful, uncomplicated days when Bonnie and Cliff had first taken her into their home. Jake had popped in often in those days, even though he was working long hours, saving up to go overseas for more experience. His impromptu visits to Bonnie's had been the highlight of Lexie's day, even though he'd loved to tease her, and kid around. He'd seemed to get a kick out of baiting her.

He was already a brilliant photo-journalist, much in demand in Australia, not just in Sydney but interstate as well. But he'd been determined to make a name for himself in Europe and America. The tough overseas experience was necessary for any photographer wanting to be an international success.

Finally the dreaded time of parting had come. The day before he was due to leave he'd dropped in to Bonnie's to say goodbye.

'I'll be grown-up by the time you come back,' she remembered complaining to him after he'd warned her that he might be away for years.

'Maybe that's the idea,' had been his drawling response.

'What do you mean?' Her eyes had flown to his in hurt indignation, but he'd simply smiled and shrugged off the question.

'You think I'm just a kid!' she'd said, pouting. At sixteen, the thought of Jake still looking on her as a child had really rankled.

She'd idolised him in those days. Worshipped the ground he walked on. And dreamily imagined that one day he would see her as more than just a long-legged schoolkid—an abandoned waif he'd rescued and dumped on his aunt and uncle—and fall for her the way she'd fallen for him.

She wistfully recalled Jake's response to her outburst.

'If that were true,' he'd murmured softly, 'why would I drop in here so often to see you?'

'For Aunt Bonnie's home cooking!' she'd shot back, but her dark eyes had pleaded with him to deny it.

He'd merely grinned.

'I knew it!' she cried, fury and hurt showing in her eyes.

'Maybe you could take a few lessons from her,' Jake teasingly suggested.

'I already am,' she said smugly, jutting out her chin. 'I've asked Bonnie to teach me how to cook so I can give her a hand with her home-catering business. I'm already helping her at weekends, delivering meals.'

'Lexie, that's great, but I'm sure my aunt would never want or expect any repayment. She's always telling me what a delight it is to have you in the family. She always wanted a daughter.' Jake eyed her quizzically. 'Maybe she's hoping you'll give up the idea of becoming a journalist and become a partner in her home-catering business instead.'

'Give up journalism?' Lexie looked shocked. 'Never!' Jake had asked her months earlier what she wanted to be when she grew up and she'd answered unthinkingly, 'A wife and mother.' When he'd pointed out that it might be an idea to have a career or a job first, she'd decided on the spot, in a blinding flash of inspiration, that she would be a journalist—a top-flight journalist—because that way she could work side by side with Jake one day, writing articles to go with his brilliant photographs, maybe even travel with him on assignments, not just here in Australia, but all over the world.

'My English teacher says I'm good enough to go to the very top!' she told Jake with a toss of her glossy black hair.

'OK, OK, just testing you,' Jake said mildly, tweaking her cheek.

'Oh, you!' She started pummelling him with her fists, and he laughingly caught her wrists and jerked her hard up against him.

'Hit me, would you?' he growled through his laughter, his warm breath fanning her flushed face.

She looked up at him breathlessly, her heart beating a hundred to the second, her soft lips parting. Then suddenly he swooped his head down and kissed her full on the mouth, a quick, hard kiss. Before she had time to react, it was over. He snapped his head back as if her lips had scalded him—or *poisoned* him?—and almost flung her away from him.

'Go back to your homework, you little minx! I have to get back to work.'

'Jake, don't be cross with me!' she shrieked after him. 'I'm sorry I hit you! I—I won't do it again!'

'Neither will I,' he said grimly, but he raised a hand in a conciliatory gesture as he strode from the house without looking back.

The next day Jake flew off to Europe. Devastated as she was, she knuckled down to her studies, determined to achieve the high marks she needed to get into university and study journalism. As a top-class journalist she would be worthy of Jake, would make him proud of her. Wherever he had to go, she would be prepared to go. She would make herself indispensable to him!

Until one day, she hoped with all her heart, he would decide to settle down at last and marry her. They would buy a home of their own, back here in Australia, and start having babies…lots of babies. She would have what she had dreamed of all her life. The man she loved and children of her own. A home. A *family*. With Jake.

She didn't realise she'd made a choking sound until Jake touched her hand.

'So you do miss him, then, Lexie?' he asked quietly, a touch of sympathy in his voice for the first time.

She blinked and looked up at him. For a second she wondered who he was talking about. As she jerked back to reality and realised where she was, a tide of heat rose up her throat into her cheeks.

'I—' She gulped, not knowing how to answer. She couldn't lie to him. Not about this. 'I miss the old Dominic,' she said carefully. 'The way he used to be.'

It seemed so long ago now. As an affectionate older brother, during the time she was living with Bonnie and Cliff, and, later, as a proud new husband, Dominic had been so different, so gentle and amiable and content with his life.

When she had first come into his family he'd been about to go off to university to study engineering, with a view to joining the Thorn family's thriving engineering business and taking over the reins one day from his father and uncle. He'd come home most weekends, and he'd spent most of his holidays at home, so she'd seen quite a bit of him in the four long years that she'd waited for Jake to come home from overseas.

During those years she'd only seen Jake twice, when he'd flown home for Bonnie and Cliff's silver wedding anniversary and, a year later, for his father's funeral.

Dominic had always been as different from Jake as chalk and cheese. Where Jake, with his tough, rough-diamond good looks and startling blue eyes, had stolen her heart in an instant, Dominic had left her unmoved in any romantic sense, despite being better looking in the classical sense and nearer to her own age.

She had looked on him as a kindly older brother, nothing more. A brother she could talk to and confide in. And Dominic, knowing how she felt about Jake, had buried his own less than brotherly feelings—as he'd confessed to her later—in the hope that, with Jake out of her sight and out of her reach for years on end, she would eventually forget his roving, daredevil cousin and start noticing him instead.

'So he *had* changed...as Bonnie said.' Jake's voice stirred her from her thoughts. Feeling his eyes on her, she stared at the hands in her lap, inspecting her fingers as if checking for broken fingernails.

'I'd rather forget it...not talk about it,' she muttered. 'I want to spare Bonnie and Cliff any more pain.'

'Maybe it would help them if they knew *why* he'd changed?' Jake suggested levelly. 'As his wife, Lexie, you must have some idea.'

She shook her head, letting her hands flutter in the air. 'Please, Jake—'

'Was it me, Lexie?' Jake's voice roughened. 'Was he worried that you still...had some feeling for me? That you didn't love him...the way he loved you?'

She reacted violently, leaping from her chair. 'You have such an ego, Jake!' Her voice was a ragged gasp. 'You think that any woman who's loved you once must forever be pining for you. Well, you're wrong! Dominic was well aware that I'd loved you before I—before we got together, and he didn't care. He knew that was all over.'

'Over? That wasn't the impression I got when I left you to go to the Amazon,' Jake reminded her, bitterness hardening his voice.

She felt panic rising inside her. 'Dominic offered me what you never could,' she choked out. 'A home. A family. Love. He loved me to the day he died. And I…I loved him! If he'd changed…it had nothing to do with you!'

She spun away from him, knowing full well that it had. Even though Sam had been the unfortunate focus of Dominic's dark moods, Sam and Jake had rolled into one in her husband's tortured mind.

She stumbled to the door, mumbling, 'I think I can hear Sam!' and nearly collided with Mary in the doorway. The child wasn't with her.

'Sam's awake, but he refuses to come out.' Mary's brown eyes showed concern. 'He heard voices, you see. I told him it was his uncle Jake's voice he could hear, but he still won't come out. You know how shy he's been lately…especially with men.'

'He's probably not properly awake yet. I'll go and see.' Lexie swept past her, without glancing back at Jake.

Sam was sitting hunched into a ball at the end of his bed, his small, dimpled arms wrapped round his bent knees, his big black eyes fixed on the open door as Lexie walked in.

'How's my boy?' she said brightly. 'It's all right, pet, Mummy's home again.' She sat on the bed and pulled him into her arms. 'Your…uncle Jake's come to visit us. He's flown all the way from Africa. You remember your uncle Jake…Nana and Grandpa have told you about him…about the famous photographs he takes all over the world, and the exciting white-water races he's won in his kayak.

They've shown you some of his photographs in magazines. You've seen a picture of him, too. In the jungle, remember?'

'Well, I'm glad to hear I'm not a complete stranger to my young cousin,' Jake's voice drawled from behind.

As she flicked a startled look around, she felt Sam shrink back against her, as if afraid that Jake was going to swoop down and tear him away from her.

'It's all right, darling.' She gave the boy a quick hug, aware of the heightened heat in her cheeks. 'You don't need to be shy, pet. It's your uncle Jake. You remember seeing his African pictures, don't you?' She gave a tiny shiver. Bonnie had shown the boy Jake's published articles from time to time, but one article in particular… No, best not to mention that one. Sam might remember how it had rebounded on them both at the time. 'Remember the one of the big waterfall?' she asked instead. 'Do you remember what it was called?'

Sam shook his head, his unblinking gaze on Jake.

'Go on…you can remember,' Lexie prompted, kissing the top of his head. 'The Victoria Falls! Now do you remember?'

'So…' Jake took a step closer. 'Your mum has shown you some of the work I do, has she?' Though his eyes were on Sam, Lexie knew that he was really speaking to her. He was surprised that she'd bothered to mention him at all, let alone show off his work.

'Well, you are a close relative,' she reminded him, looking at her son, not at Jake. She'd encouraged Sam to look at Jake's pictures whenever Bonnie had proudly pointed out a new article of Jake's in some magazine or newspaper. She had wanted Sam to know that Jake existed, to have some knowledge of the man who had fathered him, some idea of what Jake was doing with his life, and where he was…if only as a remote, footloose 'uncle'.

'Not that we've heard much news of you these past few years,' she added, trying to keep any lingering resentment from her voice. When had they ever? In the two years he had been away battling the Amazon single-handed, they hadn't heard a word. And any news that she and Dominic had heard of him in these past three years had come to them through Bonnie and Cliff…and even then it had been little more than snippets, a passing mention, or a casually displayed magazine article. Dominic had always been touchy about any mention of Jake, and Bonnie and Cliff had been fully aware that *she* hadn't welcomed reminders of Jake Thorn.

'There didn't seem much point,' Jake said, showing a glimpse of his own bitterness, his own deep scars. 'Besides which, I haven't often been in a position to communicate.' He smiled down at Sam, explaining, 'I spend a lot of my time in lonely, far-off parts of the world—in the wilds— where you don't normally find a phone or a mail box.' He lifted his gaze to Lexie's face. 'Nice to know you've told my cousin something about me.'

Lexie tried to keep her voice level as she countered with a careless shrug, 'I thought he should know why his uncle Jake never came to visit him…and the kind of work that kept him away.' Her chin lifted imperceptibly. 'Naturally your name came up from time to time. Bonnie and Cliff are still very fond of you, you know.' As for their son…with his increasing paranoia over the past three years, Dominic would have been glad if he'd never heard Jake Thorn's name again.

'They're both fond of you, too, Lexie,' Jake reminded her, a grimness in the line of his mouth. 'I'd think twice, if I were you, about leaving them in the lurch, with no-body.'

'I'm not—' she began, and clamped her mouth shut. Jake didn't understand that she was thinking of *them*, considering *their* feelings, that she was trying to do the right thing by moving away, becoming independent of them. She had to show them that she could stand on her own two feet. So that later, when they learnt the truth about Sam...

'I can't stay on here in this house,' she said tightly. 'Or in Baulkham Hills. Look, it's not as if I'll be in another city or another state. I'll just—I'll just be moving a bit closer to town.' She rose from the bed, lifting Sam in her arms as she stood up. 'I must give Sam his bath, and his tea. Why don't you go over to Bonnie and Cliff's, Jake? They wanted to see you, remember? Stay and have dinner with them. You can catch up with some of your relatives at the same time.'

He looked down at her, an expression she couldn't read intensifying the blue of his eyes. 'Won't you and Sam come with me?'

She thought of the eager relatives, clustering around Jake, welcoming home the family hero, the world-famous photo-journalist, the daredevil adventurer, and shook her head.

'No...you go, Jake.' Maybe he might even decide to stay there overnight. He must be used to sleeping on floors. Far worse places, probably. 'I...I'd like to spend some time with Sam, and then have an early night.' She needed time to think. To ponder on what she should do. About Sam.

About Jake.

'Then give me a key so I won't disturb you when I come back in.'

Jake was looking into her face as if searching for something. But his own expression was inscrutable.

CHAPTER FOUR

LEXIE was in bed, still lying awake, when she heard Jake let himself in the front door. All her nerve-ends sprang upright as he tiptoed past her bedroom door to his own room down the passage. She held her breath as she heard him come out again a moment later. Sounds came from the bathroom opposite his room, followed by muffled foot-steps going back again. She heard the creak of his bed-springs as he lowered himself down on the bed.

Even with her own door firmly closed, she felt vulner-able and exposed, knowing he was so close, knowing he was lying in his bed with only a thin wall between them. What was he wearing? Pyjamas? Or…nothing?

Her cheeks flamed in the darkness. She began to trem-ble, and then, despite herself, to fantasise, her mind con-juring up a vivid image of him stealing naked into her room…pausing a moment by her bed…bending down… touching her.

She arched her back, squirming at the erotic, sensual thoughts crowding into her mind. How she'd missed Jake's strongly muscled arms around her, she realised now. How she'd missed his passionate kisses, his lovemaking…even though he'd only ever made love to her that one time. And even then he'd been fighting against it. He hadn't meant to lose control; it had just…happened.

She had never felt those heady, erotic sensations with Dominic.

Dominic… She winced in the darkness. She'd tried so hard to love Dominic the way she'd always loved Jake…to feel the same response to his lovemaking that she'd felt in Jake's arms. But Dominic had never been a particularly sensitive or virile lover; he'd always been too abrupt, too impatient to get her pregnant with his own child. His lovemaking had left her unsatisfied, frustrated, barely roused. Whereas Jake...

She let out a deep sigh, and realised that she was becoming aroused even now, just knowing that Jake was so close, knowing that he was lying only a few metres away from her in his own bed...perhaps even thinking similar thoughts about *her*.

If only...

If only they could go back in time...back to that hot, steamy November day five years ago, the happiest and worst day of her life, and start all over again...

She sighed, a moan slipping from her lips at the memory of that bitter-sweet day. Jake's last day at home before flying off to South America to achieve his lifelong ambition—his dream—of kayaking solo down the mighty Amazon river from its remotest branch. A top international magazine had already commissioned his story and photographs. Wealthy sponsors were backing him. It was something that no man on his own had ever done before. There had been attempts, but all had failed. Many were calling it a suicidal venture.

Jake had driven her to a quiet cove near Palm Beach for the day. They'd packed a picnic lunch to eat on the beach. He'd been in high spirits, determined to make their last day together a happy one, a day to remember.

But all she'd been able to think about was that he was leaving her again...perhaps this time going off to his death. She'd wanted their day alone together to be so special, so memorable, that Jake would blurt out how he really felt about her and maybe, just maybe, even change his mind about leaving her for the madness he had in mind. She'd been so scared for him…a lone man, attempting to conquer the Amazon in a flimsy kayak, just to prove it could be done. That *he* could do it.

She'd been just twenty-one. Her girlish infatuation for Jake had long since deepened to love, and her love for him had strengthened even more in the weeks he'd been home from overseas, preparing for his hazardous adventure.

And Jake felt the same—she'd been sure of it. She had seen the look in his eyes when he'd first come home, his piercing blue gaze raking over her, almost devouring her from head to toe. She'd seen that same look many times in the weeks since. For the first time since she'd known him, Jake had been looking at her with the eyes of a man looking at a woman. It was what she had longed for from the moment she'd first met him.

There'd been a new respect in his eyes too. She'd gained poise and confidence since she'd been at university studying journalism and, having recently won a rare cadetship with a major newspaper, she'd been rapidly acquiring extra knowledge and experience. Jake's pride in her had shone from his eyes.

Since he'd been back home, they'd spent all their spare time together, talking, laughing, joking, growing closer, getting to know each other in every way but one. Jake would often hold her, touch her, gaze tenderly into her eyes. He would even kiss her long and lingeringly. But he'd never gone beyond a certain point…never spoken of love or of a future together—other than to talk vaguely of a working partnership at some time in the future, once he'd got the Amazon out of his system.

It was as if he was deliberately holding something of himself back. As if he didn't want her to be too tied to him…emotionally.

In case he didn't come back? There was no doubt he would be facing terrible, untold dangers. Possibly even death.

She stirred restlessly in her bed as memories of their last day together flooded back, still as clear as crystal in her mind. The seagulls circling the beach. The surf rolling in and crashing on to the shore. The swirl of fizzing white foam spreading over the sun-drenched sand. The tiny cove had been deserted. They'd had it all to themselves.

As she'd stripped down to her new hot-pink bikini, she could still feel Jake watching her, feel his eyes searing over her as if intent on memorising every curve, every slender bone and hollow, every inch of her. Her long black hair streamed in a glossy fall down her milky-white back, the bright sunlight picking out dazzling blue-black highlights.

When she spread her towel on the soft white sand and lowered herself down on her back, slipping the straps of her bikini top from her shoulders, she felt Jake's eyes riveted on the exposed swell of her breasts, before he snapped them away.

'Hell, Lexie, don't make it any harder for me to leave you!' His voice thickened, sounding so unlike his usual soft, teasing drawl. 'I'm going for a swim.'

As he strode off, her eyes drank in the sight of him in his brief black swimming-trunks, his magnificent body as bronzed and muscular as a Greek god, his long stride a harmony of lithe grace and power. He was like a beautiful untamed animal.

Would she ever have any hope of taming him?

When she ran down to the surf to join him, Jake began body-surfing the incoming waves like a man possessed. Whenever she came too close, he avoided looking at her, avoided touching her. Not, she sensed, because he didn't want to, but because he didn't dare. He didn't want a heavy, emotional involvement. Other things were more important to him.

But, Jake, her heart cried, I need to know how much I mean to you!

In desperation, she plunged after him as he body-surfed to shore on a bigger-than-usual wave, somehow managing to land on top of him as the wave exploded on the beach in a tumbling froth of white. Shrieking with wild laughter, she clung to his neck, her slender legs tangling with his strong thighs as they rolled over and over in the bubbling, seething foam, wrapped in each other's arms.

For a long, thrilling moment Jake clasped her tightly to him. Then he groaned, 'If we stay like this I won't be responsible for the consequences! Come on, you little minx, let's go and have lunch.'

Before she released him, she caught his face in both hands and pulled it down to meet hers. Then she kissed him, full on the lips. Hard. As she exulted at the leap of desire in his eyes, at the muffled sound in his throat, she rolled away from him and raced up the beach, drops of water spraying from her flowing hair and running down her creamy legs as she ran.

She was glowingly aware that Jake was watching every step she took. It gave her a giddy sense of elation, a surge of shivery excitement. He wanted her as much as she wanted him. She'd just seen it in his eyes. He was trying his best not to give in to it, not to lose control.

Did it—could it—mean that he *loved* her as well as desired her?

If he did, how could he bear to leave her, bear to risk his life battling a wildly dangerous, untamed river? How could he bear to stay away from her for *years*, as he'd already warned her was possible?

If she told him she loved *him*, and begged him to stay…would he?

She seized her chance after they'd eaten their picnic lunch and packed things away.

'Mmm…that lunch you and Bonnie prepared was yummy. Scrumptious.' Jake straightened, smiling down at her in a way that made her bones dissolve. 'I won't get food like that where I'm going.'

She raised stark eyes to his, a shiver gliding down her spine. 'Jake, I'm so afraid for you! Don't go…please don't go!' The plea burst from her. 'It's going to be so terribly dangerous! I couldn't bear it if anything happened to you!' She realised she was clinging to him, the soft curves of her body straining against the whipcord leanness of his.

She felt his body stiffen at the contact. 'Nothing is going to happen to me, Lexie,' he assured her a trifle huskily, his hand circling gently over her shoulder blades. 'I know what I'm doing. I've been riding rapids in my spare time for years. Some of the wildest rivers in the world. I won't be taking any unnecessary risks, believe me.'

'But Dominic says people have *died* attempting to do what you plan to do!' The whole crazy venture was a risk! An insane, death-defying risk from start to finish. *If* he finished!

Jake's mouth tightened at the mention of his cousin, his eyes glinting into hers, electric-blue slits in his deeply tanned face. 'Maybe that's what he's hoping…so that *he* can move in on you!'

Her eyes sprang wide. 'Dominic? He's like a brother to me!'

'Give him half a chance and he'd soon forget about being brotherly!' Jake grated. 'I've seen the way he looks at you. Pathetic puppy dog!'

She lifted her chin, a taunting gleam in her eyes. 'Jealous, Jake? Maybe that's another reason you should stay at home. To stop Dominic stealing me away from you!'

For a fleeting second, a dark glow kindled in his eyes. His grip tightened on her arms, his fingers digging deep into her flesh. 'My insipid cousin?' His lips curled. 'Dominic's not man enough for a handful like you.'

'Oh, no?' An elated spark lit her eyes. So he did care! She tossed back her head, her black hair tumbling in a gleaming wave over her bare shoulders. 'At least *he'd* never go off into the wilds and leave a girl he cared about for years on end, without even promising to keep in touch! Without even telling her how he feels about her! Aren't you even going to…kiss me goodbye, Jake? A proper kiss goodbye?'

Jake sucked in a deep breath. 'Lexie, don't tempt me.' He seemed to be doing his desperate best not to meet her eyes…or look down at her body.

'*Tempt* you, Jake?' If only she could! Perhaps, if she showed him how *she* felt…

She flicked the tip of her tongue over her soft lips and wriggled closer, brushing her hips seductively against his.

'Lexie, no!' he groaned, stepping back. He held her at arm's length. 'Don't touch me!'

'You don't even want me to *touch* you?' she whispered, looking up at him uncertainly, her eyes pained.

He swore. 'Lexie, what I want and what I think is best for you are two different things! For pity's sake, let's get back to the—'

'You *don't* want me!' It was a cry of hurt. 'You're glad you're going away! You've *never* wanted me. Not the way I want you!'

'Wanting has nothing to do with it,' he muttered thickly. 'It's what it could lead to that—'

He gritted his teeth. As she gazed tremulously up at him

his chest heaved in a heavy sigh. 'You just get on with your studies and your work at the paper, Lexie.' He glared down at her, a smouldering hardness in his eyes. 'I'm not going away leaving you all dewy-eyed and lovesick, mooning over me, feeling committed to me, putting your life on hold for me. I want to know that you're getting on with your life. Damn it, I don't even know if I—' He stopped, hissing in a savage breath.

'If you *will* be back?' she finished for him, clutching at his arm in terror. 'Jake, I'm already dewy-eyed and love-sick…sick with love for *you!*' The admission tumbled out. 'So it's no use telling me to forget you, if that's what you're trying to do.' Desperation wrenched out a further anguished appeal. 'Why can't you admit that you're in love with me too?'

She felt him flinch, saw his eyes growing flat and un-readable under her gaze. 'In love?' he jeered, his tone harsh now, laced with scorn. 'A footloose adventurer like me? I've no time for love or commitment,' he said bru-tally. 'I need to concentrate my mind on what I'll be doing. And you should be doing the same, Lexie. You have your career to think of. Your studies. A lot of living to do. I'm going to be away for a long time. I want you to get on with your life, enjoy it. Knowing you're *free* to enjoy it. Hell, Lexie, you're only twenty-one!'

'I'm a grown woman, Jake,' she asserted vehemently. 'And I know what I want. I want *you*, Jake. I *love* you. Nothing's going to change that, no matter how long you're away from me.' As she spoke she could feel him slipping away from her and a reckless desperation gripped her. 'Tell me you love me too, Jake! *Show* me! I need to know!' Intent on drawing an admission from him, she ran a provocative finger down his chest, continuing on down…lower…even lower…

'For pity's sake, Lexie—don't!' He grabbed her hand.

'Don't you like me touching you, Jake?' she whispered, her breath quickening, a honeyed weakness spreading through her limbs at the thought of touching him more intimately.

He made a choking sound in his throat, sweat breaking out on his upper lip, his eyes a shimmering blue blaze above hers. He was fast losing control and, seeing it, feeling it in the faint shuddering of his body, hearing it in his laboured breathing, she felt her own control slipping away too, her body trembling with longing, blood pulsing through her brain.

'Kiss me, Jake,' she pleaded, tilting her face to his. 'Please...' She strained against him, feeling the burning heat of her breasts as she moulded them into the sinewy contours of his naked chest, her nipples growing hard against his heated skin. 'Don't leave me like this, Jake, without—without *something*!'

His body shuddered under the eager pressure of hers, a hoarse growl rising from his throat as her lips frantically sought his.

'Hell, Lexie, you're driving me out of my mind!' He lashed his arms around her, almost bending her over backwards, his rasping breath hot on her face. 'I can't let you go now...not now!' With a tortured moan, he crushed her to him, his mouth opening, swallowing hers, his lips grinding over hers in ruthless, savage possession.

She gave a gasping sigh and gave herself up to his kisses...wild, smothering, flaming kisses that were nothing like the tender, sweetly lingering kisses they'd shared before. He snatched fierce breaths in between, his hands feverishly at work on her face, her throat, all over her silken body, his heart thundering against hers.

She moaned and gasped for air, clinging to him, straining into him, their kisses growing more frenzied as they frantically tore off the skimpy pieces of cloth that still lay between them, then sank down onto the sand, clasped in each other's arms.

They were both lost…lost in a swirl of throbbing emotion and the most explosive, piercingly exquisite sensations that Lexie had ever experienced, had ever dreamed possible.

She writhed in her bed, almost crying out as she relived those same sensations now, piquant spasms shaking her body as if Jake were making love to her right here and now. Until she realised it was just her memory playing tricks, the heady, tantalising thought of Jake in the spare bedroom next door arousing sensations so potently real, so erotic that he could have been here in the bed with her.

She gave a long, wistful sigh and fell back, the fire slowly ebbing from her body, spreading a deep, relaxing warmth through her veins.

And then she groaned as another memory from that day on the beach drifted uncomfortably back. As she remembered the dismayed look on Jake's face after the waves of passion had subsided.

'I've never lost control like that before…never been unprotected before.' He'd held her tight, his face turned tautly to hers. 'What if—?'

'Don't worry, Jake.' She couldn't bear to see the worried concern in his eyes. Was it directed at her…or himself? What if he was already regretting…?

'I'm on the pill.' The lie leapt from her lips. She wanted to ease his mind and stop him worrying about a possibility that hadn't occurred to her either until then. Not that there would be anything to worry about…not the first time…surely? 'I've been on the pill since you came home,' she assured him. A second lie slipping out.

His brow shot up. 'You knew this was going to happen?'

'No!' She flushed. 'But loving you, Jake, I—it seemed only sensible.' She felt so guilt-stricken lying to him, but tomorrow he was going off to the wilds of the Amazon, and she didn't want him worrying about it, fretting over it…and maybe not concentrating on what he was doing, and perhaps making a fatal error…

She choked at the thought, and cried out in fear, 'Jake, how can you leave me now…after this? I—I'm so afraid! I can't bear to think of the horrors you might be going into, of what could happen to you. I can't lose you now, Jake!' She clutched at him. 'Change your mind, Jake, *please* change your mind!' she pleaded huskily. 'It's not too late. No one will blame you. Pull out while you have the chance. Stay here at home…with me. There's plenty of work for you here in Australia. Or we could travel overseas together. Somewhere…safer.'

'Lexie, don't do this. I have to go. It's what I've always wanted to do. I *have* to do it. It's all arranged…'

'Then take me with you!' she begged. 'I'm a journalist now, remember? I could travel with the land crew and meet you from time to time. I could write the—'

'No!' He caught her hands, being careful to hold her away from him. 'You'd be too much of a distraction. Knowing you were so close would wreck my concentration.' He swore under his breath. 'This is precisely why I didn't want this to happen. I need to feel *free*, Lexie. I can't be continually thinking about you, dreaming of you, not keeping my mind on what I'm doing.

'Let me go, Lexie,' he demanded roughly. 'Forget this ever happened. Get on with your life.' He let her go abruptly, and turned away. 'Come on...I'm taking you home.'

There was nothing more she could do. She nodded meekly, and said no more about him staying at home, or taking her with him, or about the fears she felt. The next day she bravely waved him off without a tear in her eyes...although they flowed freely enough after he'd gone.

Remembering now, Lexie gave a long, quivering sigh. *Oh, Jake... Jake... Can we ever put things right?* She rolled over with a groan and at long last, emotionally exhausted, she fell asleep.

Only to be woken with a start some time later, aroused from her sleep by shrill, piercing screams. Blood-chilling screams.

Sam!

CHAPTER FIVE

LEXIE shot out of bed and leapt for the door, barely conscious of her feet touching the floor as she flew to her son's room across the passage.

The child was sitting bolt upright in bed, his big black eyes the size of saucers, his face stark white in the soft glow of the night-lamp beside his bed. He was screaming as if he couldn't stop, his small pink mouth gaping wide. As Lexie rushed to gather him in her arms, the high-pitched screams gave way to deep, choking sobs.

'Mummy! Mummy! Mummy! Don't leave me!'

The piteous cries tore at her heart. 'It's all right, love, it's all right,' she crooned, rocking him in her arms. 'Mummy won't leave you. You've had a bad dream, but it's gone now.' As she brushed his clammy brow with a soothing hand, she used her other to gently stroke his shaking, convulsing body. 'It's all right now, pet. Mummy's here.'

But no amount of soothing or rocking seemed to help, his racking sobs growing, if anything, even more anguished, punctuated with choked, incoherent mumbles. Lexie, murmuring soft words of comfort as she cradled him in her arms, was at a loss to know what to do. He'd had nightmares before, but never like this.

'Darling, tell Mummy,' she pleaded. 'Tell me what's wrong.'

It was obvious he was trying to tell her something, but his words so far were unintelligible.

'I didn't hear you, darling. Tell me again. Slowly…take it slowly. It's all right, pet, nothing can hurt you now.'

The child took a deep. shuddering breath. 'He—he was ch-chasing me,' he gulped out. 'And—and shouting at me.'

She went cold. 'It was just a bad dream, darling. Nobody is chasing you. Nobody is *going* to chase you.'

'But he d-did! He *will*! He'll get me, I know he will!'

Lexie's heart turned to ice. She took a deep breath and whispered, 'Who'll get you, darling?'

Sam clung to her, gasping between sobs, '*He* will! D-Daddy! It's m-my fault he's dead; it's all my fault!' With a long, plaintive wail, he buried his face in her shoulder.

Her eyes snapped wide in shock. 'Darling, no!' she cried, hugging him tight. 'Of course it wasn't your fault. Daddy had an accident. On some iron stairs at work. His foot slipped and he fell. You had nothing to do with it.'

'Yes, I did! I *did*! I s-said to him—' he screwed up his face '—"I wish you were dead!"'

'Oh, my poor baby!' She pressed her lips to his soft damp cheek. 'You were just cross. You were upset. You didn't mean it. Daddy knew you didn't.'

'But I did! I d-did mean it!' Renewed sobs racked his tiny body.

Lexie felt a knife-sharp pain pierce her heart. 'There, there, darling; it's all right, truly, love. We all say silly things when we're cross with someone, but it's only words. Words can't hurt people. What happened to Daddy was an *accident*, darling…it had nothing to do with you,' she stressed, rocking him gently in her arms as she stroked the damp hair back from his face. She went on murmuring soft, consoling words until at last the choking sobs began to subside.

Then she heard another sound. From behind. 'Here,'

said a deep, calm voice, and a hand thrust a glass of water at her. 'Give him this.'

She raised startled eyes, and met Jake's. Her heart gave a sharp jump, part apprehension, part dismay. How long had he been standing there, listening? He was wearing only boxer shorts, his tanned chest bare, all smooth, hard muscle. She tried not to look at him.

'Thanks,' she mumbled, gratitude overriding her unease. She took the glass of water from him and urged Sam to take a sip. Jake was simply being thoughtful. Compassionate. She'd missed that in recent months—having a thoughtful, compassionate man around.

Not that it would be for long.

She kept her eyes on Sam's ravaged face, burying a flare of resentment at the thought of Jake vanishing from her life again in a few days' time. When, for that matter, had Jake Thorn's compassion ever lasted for any length of time? He'd never been one for considering other people...their needs, their wishes, their feelings. Not in the long term. He'd never been *around* for long enough.

But that was unfair... She swallowed. There had been a time...

She felt Sam stir in her arms, saw him glance warily up at Jake. Feeling his small body stiffen, she said quickly, handing the half-empty glass back to Jake, 'Thanks, Jake. I'm sure he'll be all right now. I'll just stay with him until he goes back to sleep.'

'Right.' Jake smiled down at Sam, but made no attempt to touch him, or move closer. 'Good night, tiger. See you in the morning. If you like, I'll show you some photographs I brought back from Africa. I think you might like the ones of the baby gorilla. He's a cute little guy.'

Sam didn't answer, but his head moved slightly, in what looked like a faint nod.

As Lexie settled the boy down, Jake disappeared from the room as soundlessly as he'd come.

About twenty minutes later, as she tiptoed across the passage to her own room, Jake's voice halted her.

'He's OK now?' His tall frame took shape out of the gloom of the passage...as if he'd been waiting, listening out for her.

Now that Sam was asleep again and no longer an immediate concern, she felt suddenly self-conscious as she faced Jake in the dimness, aware that she wore only a short, flimsy nightie. The only light came from Jake's room down the passage, but it was enough to make her aware again of his semi-naked state. And her own.

'He's fast asleep,' she whispered. 'Thanks for—'

'Let's talk in here.' With his hand on her arm he swept her into her bedroom, somehow finding the lamp by her bed and switching it on.

As he turned to face her, she swallowed. Now she felt more vulnerable and exposed than ever, acutely aware of his smooth, sun-bronzed chest, his sleep-tousled hair, his raw masculinity. Acutely aware of her own state of undress, her brief nightie showing far too much leg and so sheer it was almost transparent.

'Come and sit down for a moment.' He waved a hand. On the bed, he plainly meant. The only chair in the room stood over by the window.

As she hesitated, Jake lowered himself down on her crumpled duvet, patting the space beside him. 'We need to talk.'

'Now?' She heard the dismay in her voice, and said quickly, 'Jake, I'm sorry we disturbed you, but...I need my sleep. So must you. Can't it wait until morning? All I want to do right now is—'

'*Now*, Lexie.' She'd heard that implacable tone before.

'In the morning you'll have Sam with you and I don't want to talk about this in front of him.'

Her mouth went dry. 'Talk about what?' she asked, sinking carefully down onto the bed beside him...not too close.

'I want to know what's been going on in this house between you and Sam and Dominic. Why Sam would wish his father dead. Why the boy's having nightmares that his father is chasing him. Why you, Lexie, are not showing the usual signs of the distressed, mourning widow.'

Lexie felt alarm tugging at her throat. If she opened up even a little, Jake would want to know everything. And she couldn't...mustn't...not yet.

'Jake, it was just a bad dream. A small child's guilty conscience.' She gulped hard. 'You heard him. He got angry with Dominic one day...the way all children get angry with their parents at some time or other. They say things they don't mean. How often have you heard a child shout, "I wish you were dead"? If Dominic hadn't...died, Sam would never have thought any more about it. None of us would.'

'What made him so angry with Dominic in the first place?' Jake persisted, frowning. His strong thighs, thrusting like sturdy tree-trunks from his striped boxer shorts, were evoking disturbing memories in Lexie's mind...as disturbing as this conversation.

'I don't know.' She shrugged, clasping her hands tightly in her lap. Avoiding Jake's eyes. 'I suppose Dominic must have growled at him. Maybe Sam had left his toys lying around,' she improvised. 'It doesn't take much to make a sensitive child feel—'

'Did Dominic often lose his temper with Sam?' Jake sliced in.

She flicked a nervous tongue over her lips. 'No more than—than most fathers. Dominic—' She hesitated, biting her lip. 'He'd been a bit—a bit touchy. Moody. As Bonnie told you. Jake, I—'

'Did he ever hit Sam?' Jake asked abruptly.

'No!' Her eyes flew to his face. It had been her greatest fear, though…that one day he might.

'Well, what was going on, then?' Jake demanded, his rugged face grim in the lamp's soft glow. 'You might have fooled Bonnie and Cliff into believing you had no idea what was eating into your husband, Lexie, but you can't fool me. You know, don't you? I can sense it, see it in the way you're avoiding my eye. I know you pretty well, remember? Probably better than anyone.'

'You?' she scorned, seizing on anger to hide the quick apprehension she felt inside. 'You know nothing about me! You haven't been near me—near any of us—for years!'

'There was hardly much point, was there? Once I found out you'd married Dominic.' The reminder came with an ironic lift of his lip. 'But you never loved him, did you, Lexie? Oh, you might have played the role of the devoted, dutiful wife, I'll grant you that. I saw you three years ago, remember, and you played your part to the hilt, doing your level best to convince me that you were happy with Dominic and had everything you'd ever wanted. But the second we were alone…the second I touched you—'

'*Stop it!*' She leapt off the bed, and gasped as he halted her with a snap of his hand around her wrist.

'OK. Bad timing. I'm sorry.' His tone was penitent. But only just. 'Lexie, I'm not saying you didn't try. That you let him down in any way…'

Oh, but she had! If she'd been able to give Dominic a child…his *own* child…

'I did love Dominic!' she choked out. It might never have been the passionate, helpless, all-consuming love she'd felt for Jake. But she *had* loved him…at one time.

In the beginning as a brother, and later as a dear friend, a valued confidant. She'd even loved him as a caring husband and father...at least for the first year or so of their marriage, when he'd still been his old self and had seemed to care about Sam.

Dominic had loved *her* so much that he'd been willing to love her child too, and bring him up as his own son. Until Jake had reappeared, two years later, disturbing his peace of mind...and hers...and sparking off the paranoia in Dominic that was to grow and grow until...

She realised Jake was eyeing her sceptically, and flushed, conceding, 'All right, I might not have loved him the way I once loved you. One's first love is always the love of one's life, don't they say? Explosive, unforgettable, all passion and intense emotion.' Her tone was derisive, dismissive. 'But it doesn't necessarily go—go deep.' *Oh, no?* 'Or—or last.'

She tried to withdraw her hand as she spoke, but Jake's fingers only tightened their grip on her wrist. She went on, resolving to ignore it. 'With Dominic, it—' She paused, dragging in her breath. 'It was a gentler, calmer sort of love. The type that's more...enduring.' It might have endured too, in its calm, gentle way, if Dominic hadn't become so obsessed, so paranoid about Sam, about the truth coming out...or if she had given him a child of his own.

Or if Jake had never come back into their lives.

Jake gave a brief, harsh laugh. 'You're a passionate creature, Lexie, and you always will be. You need passion in your life as much as you need air.'

She flinched. She didn't want to talk about passion or needs. Earlier tonight—thankfully in the privacy of her own bed—she had realised that she was still susceptible to Jake. Far too susceptible.

'I was a good wife to Dominic,' she asserted. 'A loving,

faithful wife. Just because I reacted to *you* that one time…'
She shivered, feeling a reaction even now, Jake's hard grip
on her wrist sending tiny shocks of heated awareness
through her. 'It was just an—an instinctive physical reaction. I suppose because I'd been so—so smitten with
you…once.' She tossed her head in a gesture of defiance.
'Dominic did give me everything I'd ever wanted. A home
of my own. A family. A feeling of security and permanence. He was a—a wonderful husband, a wonderful person…' She trailed off, swallowing hard. Until his mind
became warped with his insidious fears, and soured by his
failure to make me pregnant, she added silently.

'You didn't mention happiness,' Jake said wryly. '*Were*
you happy with him, Lexie?'

As she chewed on her lip, her eyes misting at the memory of the final tense months of a marriage gone bitterly
awry, Jake added more gently, 'Please…sit down, Lexie.'
He drew her back, not relinquishing his hold on her wrist
until she sank back down on the bed with a sigh.

'Jake, *please*,' she begged. 'I've got to get some sleep.'

'In a minute.' He turned to face her, his eyes narrowing,
searching hers. 'I want you to tell me, Lexie…' His tone
was like soft velvet now, his manner less confrontational.
'What happened to Dominic—or was it something that
happened between the two of you—to make him so moody
and depressed? Whatever it was, I can see it's still eating
into you. Or something is. And it's tormenting your son,
causing him nightmares. Get it off your chest, Lexie. Tell
me! A problem shared…'

She gave a deep, shuddering sigh. Obviously he wasn't
going to rest until he had some answers. She would have
to tell him something. A little…but not too much.

'I blame myself.' She forced the words out, unconsciously rubbing her wrist where his fingers had dug into her tender flesh.

'Why, Lexie?' Jake encouraged gently as she bowed her head, letting her silky black hair veil her face. 'Was it anything to do with…you and me?'

Her head jerked up, her dark eyes flashing, the old wounds gaping open as his assumption, whether true or not, touched her on the raw. In a flare of bitterness, she burst out shakily, 'You've never forgiven me, have you, Jake, for marrying Dominic so soon after you left? Even though you never wanted me yourself…except maybe as a—as a working partner some day, trailing around the world after you. And you didn't even want me as that when you went off to the Amazon and left me behind.'

'That's unfair, Lexie, and you know it. I couldn't take you with me…not on that trip. Even if I'd let you join my land crew, you wouldn't have seen much of me, and rarely at close quarters, let alone by ourselves. And just knowing you were there—' He grimaced. 'I needed all my wits about me, my mind concentrated on what I was doing, not on *you*, Lexie. Besides, you had your studies to finish, your cadetship at the newspaper…'

'You didn't even want to—to make love to me before you left!' The accusation burst out, a ragged cry.

He gave a brief, mirthless laugh. 'You know damned well I *wanted* to make love to you. I just didn't think it would be a good idea—taking advantage of you at such a highly charged time, the day before I left. Knowing I wouldn't be seeing you again possibly for years. I was trying to be responsible, Lexie, trying to act the gentleman, damnably hard though it was. I didn't want to leave you feeling tied to me, putting your life on hold for a—dammit, for a guy who mightn't even come back. As it was, I nearly didn't. I had some pretty hairy escapes.'

He had? She stifled a shudder. 'Jake, we're just going over old ground,' she said dully, the old guilt twisting inside her. Knowing that everything he'd said was true. Knowing that she had only herself to blame for the way they'd both lost control that day, and for the mess she'd made of her life since. Of all their lives.

Jake nodded, and gave a brief shrug. 'And we're getting off the point. You didn't answer my question, Lexie. What was bugging Dominic, making him so difficult to live with?'

'Heavens, you're persistent, Jake!' She thumped the bed with her fist. 'You seem convinced that I know!'

'You do know.' He faced her grimly. 'And you're going to tell me. I'm not leaving this room until you do. You can't keep bottling it up inside you, Lexie. It'll tear you apart.'

She sighed. 'All *right*!' Maybe he deserved to know something. She would tell him as much of the truth as she dared. As much as she thought wise...for now. Any more...well, she would have to see. Later.

'It was...' She hesitated, picking her words with care. 'It was largely frustration, I think. Since Sam was born, I—' She paused, gulping heavily before going on. 'I hadn't been able to fall pregnant again. I'd had a difficult birth, you see,' she hastened on, 'and there were... complications.'

That was true enough. But the after-effects of that long and difficult birth hadn't been permanent, as she was implying. It was Dominic's fault that they hadn't had more children. He hadn't been *able* to have children. Tests had eventually revealed the sad truth. But to tell Jake that...

Not even Bonnie knew, or Cliff. Especially not them.

She drew in a long breath. No, she couldn't tell Jake. At this point in time she didn't want Jake knowing—or

guessing—the truth about Sam's birth. To tell him would
be like pointing a gun to his head. Using emotional blackmail to keep him at home. *Stay at home here in Australia
with your child. Stay at home with me. Be what I want you
to be.* She would never do that to Jake. Once before she'd
pleaded with him to stay at home. She'd thrown herself at
him, and *begged* him to give up his dangerous, wandering
life and settle down with her.

He would think she was trying the same thing again,
using more powerful ammunition this time. His son!

No…she couldn't do it She would never use her son as
ammunition.

She took a deep breath. 'Dominic dearly wanted a
daughter,' she said truthfully, hoping that would satisfy
Jake. 'He wanted lots of children.' *Children of his own,
not another man's.* If only those children had come along,
Dominic might never… But what was the point of torturing herself about it? They *hadn't* come along, and that was
that.

'He took it out on *you*?' Jake's lip curled in disgust. 'He
couldn't be content with what he had? A healthy son and
a beautiful wife who was…devoted to him?'

Her throat suddenly felt like dust. Parched. Had she said
too much? Would he begin to wonder? Work things out?
But how could he? She'd covered her tracks too well.
Three years ago, when he'd turned up out of the blue, she
had convinced him that Sam was Dominic's child, not his.
Jake wasn't going to start doubting it now. Unless *she* put
doubts into his head. Unless she *told* him.

No, she resolved, tempted as she was to blurt out the
truth at long last. Quite apart from the emotional blackmail
angle, and the pressure it would put on Jake, she dreaded
to think how he might react. At best, he would be bitterly
hurt and angry—and rightly so. At worst, he could be so

enraged he might even try to take Sam away from her, and persuade the Thorn family—Bonnie and Cliff—to reject *her*, the way people had been rejecting and abandoning her all her life.

Even if he didn't go that far, even if he managed to bury his bitter hurt and decided to stay at home with her—even marry her, for Sam's sake—he'd be bound to end up resenting her after a while, for trapping him into a life he'd never wanted. He could end up as bitter and frustrated as Dominic had been!

Jake was bitter enough already because she'd rushed into marriage with Dominic, and tossed away a promising career in journalism instead of waiting for him to come back from the Amazon and claim her. Not claim her as his wife, of course, but as a lover and possible future travelling partner. *She* was the one who had dreamed of him one day wanting to marry her and settle down. But Jake would never want a life like that. A stable, secure, *normal* life. Not Jake.

No…far from still loving her, if he ever had, Jake must despise her now, and he would despise her even more when he knew what she had done. He might still *want* her, lust after her, but any glimmer of love he'd ever felt must have died when he'd heard she'd turned to Dominic. And it could well turn to bitter hatred when he learnt the truth about Sam.

'I need to get some sleep,' she said in a strangled voice, her slender shoulders slumping. 'Have you forgotten, Jake? I buried my husband today.'

The hand that had been resting on her back dropped away, leaving her with a sharp sense of loss, a chill deep inside. 'I guess we both do. I'm sorry, Lexie,' he said as he rose from the bed. But he didn't spell out just what he was sorry *for*. For keeping her from her sleep? For the loss of her husband? Or for the opportunities they'd both let slip away?

Could there possibly be any hope, any vague hope at all, she wondered bleakly, of other chances in the future? Or would things always be the same between them, the two of them worlds apart, emotionally and in terms of actual distance? Would the bitterness of the past and the truths yet to come out forge a fatal wedge between them?

It was Sam who woke her in the morning, creeping into her room and standing patiently by her bed until, subconsciously sensing his presence, she opened her eyes.

'Sam! Hullo, darling!' She reached out and gave him a hug. 'You're cold,' she murmured. 'Here…climb under the doona and let me warm you up.'

She pulled the duvet over him and gently rubbed his back. Mary wouldn't be back until later in the day, so he couldn't have had his breakfast yet. 'Are you hungry?' she asked with a smile.

He looked up at her with his big black eyes. 'Mummy, that man's still here.'

Her heart gave a sharp jolt. 'You mean your uncle Jake?' She forced an even brighter smile. 'You've seen him this morning?'

Sam shook his head. 'He's in the shower. I heard him. Mummy… Is he—is Uncle Jake going to be my new daddy?'

Pain pierced her heart as she saw the quick fear in his eyes. And she felt shock too, at the irony of the question. She swallowed, feeling the dryness in her throat. 'Darling, Uncle Jake is only home for a short visit. He's going to show you some of the photographs he took in Africa, remember? He's a great photographer. A great adventurer.

He goes all over the world. In a few days—' a heaviness dulled her voice '—he'll be going back to Africa.'

'Where's Africa?'

'I'll get the atlas out later and show you. Let's get dressed now, shall we? And then we'll have breakfast.'

It felt strange having Jake there sharing breakfast with them…just the three of them. Such a domestic scene. Such a family scene. Jake seemed perfectly at ease. But then, Jake was always at ease, wherever he was. Wherever in the world.

At first Sam was diffident with Jake, too shy even to speak, but when Jake produced his African photographs, especially the ones of the baby gorilla, he perked up enough to show interest in them. But he wouldn't take the photos from Jake, and he kept one eye on Lexie, not letting her out of his sight. When she told him she was going to have her shower he insisted on going to the bathroom with her, and no amount of coaxing from Jake would change his mind.

Sam stuck close by her all morning, even when the family lawyer, Wayne Caxton, called in to discuss Dominic's will.

Lexie introduced Wayne to Jake, before suggesting quickly, 'Why don't you take my car, Jake, and go over to Bonnie's?' She was afraid that Dominic might have made some revelation about Sam in his will, and she didn't want Jake finding out the truth that way. 'I'm sure she and Cliff would love to have a proper chat with you. You probably didn't get much of a chance last night, with other people there.'

She held her breath. Even if Dominic hadn't gone so far as to openly reject Sam in his will, she half expected him to have left her with nothing but the house, which was in both their names. And she didn't want Jake witnessing that either…and wondering why.

'Sure, why not?' Jake said mildly, his eyebrows lifting, as if he knew that she wanted him out of the way. 'But I won't need the car. I'll walk. How about I take Sam with me? You can follow us when you're ready. Bonnie has invited us for lunch, by the way.'

Lexie felt Sam shrinking back against her. 'You go ahead, Jake,' she urged. 'I'll bring Sam with me later in the car.'

Jake shrugged, tossed Sam a grin, and with a brief nod in Wayne Caxton's direction strode from the room.

Lexie sat Sam in front of the TV, put on one of his favourite videos to watch, then sat down at the table opposite the lawyer, who was already opening his briefcase. He unfolded the will with a flourish, and began to read.

There was no bitter repudiation of Sam. No spiteful backlash against *her*. Dominic had left her everything he possessed. The house and its contents, his money and investments, including his shares in his father's engineering business, his car…everything. If she had died first, Wayne Caxton told her, everything would have gone to Sam. 'Our son, Sam,' Dominic had written.

She felt tears stinging her eyes. She had misjudged Dominic. He hadn't hated Sam. He hadn't regretted marrying her and taking on Sam. There was no hint in his will of the demons tormenting him, of the paranoia that had been mounting daily inside him.

She swallowed hard, and buried her face in her hands. Her pain and guilt in that moment were overwhelming. She could never accept all that he'd left her. Certainly not the family shares. Or the car, which rightly belonged to the family business. It would be wrong. She didn't deserve them. She'd been planning to *leave* him.

She looked up, facing Wayne Caxton determinedly. 'Please see that the car goes to Cliff Thorn…it belongs to the company. My old station wagon is all I'll need.' It was roomy, ideal for transporting food. 'As for the shares in the Thorn Engineering Company, I…' She drew in her breath. 'They rightfully belong to Bonnie and Cliff Thorn now. His parents.'

They could do what they liked with them. Even hand them over to Jake if they wanted to. Jake might have sold his own shares three years ago, and never shown any interest in the family company in the past, but she was sure that, as he was now Bonnie and Cliff's closest living relative, they would want him to have them—in the hope that he'd keep the business going after they'd gone, even if he didn't run it himself.

The lawyer looked shocked. 'You don't want to keep those shares for your son, Mrs Thorn? Wouldn't that be what your husband would have wanted? Since it's the family company?'

She shook her head, blinking away her tears. 'I don't think so. I…I want to make a clean break, you see. Make a completely fresh start. I'll be selling this house and moving closer to the city. The memories…' She shrugged. 'I don't want any painful reminders.'

Wayne shifted uncomfortably. 'You—um—you don't feel you'd be denying your son his rightful inheritance?' he pursued delicately.

She went still. Denying him his rightful inheritance… Wasn't that precisely what she would be doing if she handed the Thorn shares back to the family? Sam was, after all, a Thorn by birth. Not *Dominic* Thorn's son but *Jake* Thorn's son. And, while he might not be the cherished grandson that Bonnie and Cliff believed him to be, he *was* their great-nephew, and always would be. Which in time they would have to know.

No. She mustn't take away from Sam what was rightfully his. Bonnie and Cliff were going to be sad enough when they heard that she and Sam were moving away from Baulkham Hills, severing the close links they'd always had, without causing them even more pain by throwing Sam's inheritance back in their faces.

And then the solution struck her. 'You're right, Wayne. Just because *I* don't want those shares…' She leaned closer. 'I want you to transfer them into my son's name. And I want his—his grandfather, Cliff Thorn, to have power of attorney. I want to have nothing more to do with them. Will you see to it?'

Wayne Caxton looked relieved. 'Certainly. If that's your wish.'

'It is.'

She broke the news to Bonnie and Cliff over lunch—that she was selling her house and moving closer to the city, and that she intended to start looking for a new house immediately.

Even though they were obviously disappointed, they took it so well that she suspected Jake must have prepared them already.

'There are two excellent up-market shopping centres with specialist cake shops that I want to be near,' she hastened to explain, without mentioning at this point that they were on the other side of the Sydney Harbour Bridge. 'They're prepared to sell any cakes I bake at home. I want to go on working from home, you see, to be with Sam. But not doing functions and dinners, as I've been doing with you, Bonnie, because it takes me away from Sam too much, especially at night. He needs me more than ever just now.'

She paused. 'There's also a possibility—' she didn't look at Jake '—of me working for a local paper in the same area. An old friend of mine who does their weekly dining-out column has asked me to fill in for her while she's overseas for a few weeks. She's due to leave next month. It'll mean going to a local restaurant once a week for dinner and writing it up.'

'But, dear,' Bonnie said gently, 'how will you manage to do that without Mary's help with Sam? Do you want Mary to come to you once a week, and stay overnight? She could keep an eye on Sam during the day, while you're busy baking.'

'Oh, Bonnie, no! It's too far—I'll be way over the other side of town—and you need her here.' Lexie's heart twisted at the older woman's generosity. 'I'll find a babysitter for the night I need to go out. And I hope to book Sam into a part-time nursery eventually, where he'll have other children to play with during the day.'

'So you'll be dining out alone at a restaurant once a week…' Jake put in silkily from his armchair across the room. 'Well, well. You never know who you might meet.'

Lexie stiffened, sensing a derisive undercurrent that made her mentally grit her teeth. He was implying that because she'd rushed into marriage once she must be on the lookout for another husband already—another father for Sam!

'I won't be dining out alone,' she said evenly. 'I'll be taking a friend.' Not *you*, Jake, her eyes told him. You'll be back in Africa by the time the job comes up. 'A *girl-friend*,' she added tartly. 'Or a neighbour. Or someone from the local paper.' She had no intention of picking up anyone, let alone a new husband.

She turned back to Bonnie, going on as if Jake hadn't intervened, 'But before I can do anything I'll have to sell my house…and look for another.'

'Well, you'll have me to help you there,' Jake drawled before Bonnie could comment. This time there was no discernible undercurrent in his voice, though she couldn't be sure. 'I've decided to stay on for a while. I might even be able to stretch my stay to a couple of weeks.'

She almost flung back, Oh, don't stretch your stay here on my account, as resentment flared through her at his reminder that he would be off again soon, for heaven knew how long this time. As if she needed reminding.

Stopping herself in time, she forced her lips into a grateful smile. Even if they had no future together as a *family*, she and Sam and Jake, she didn't want to banish Jake from her life, she realised, let alone cut him adrift from Sam. Now that Dominic had gone, Sam had lost the only father he'd ever known, and she certainly had no intention of marrying again simply to give Sam a father and a secure home and family…whatever Jake might believe.

She had to keep Jake in Sam's life…even if only as a here-today, gone-tomorrow uncle. Even if he could never be the constant father figure to Sam that she still dreamed, even now, he would be…one day.

But—she glanced at Jake's tough, deeply tanned face from under her spread of dark lashes, taking in the familiar dazzling blue of his eyes, the warm, sensual lips, the slightly crooked nose—she had to ask herself…was it only Sam she was thinking of?

CHAPTER SIX

IN THE all too short days that followed, Sam thawed more and more towards Jake, although he still made sure that either Lexie or Mary was within call. Because of the boy's disturbing nightmare on Jake's first night, and Jake's equally disturbing presence in her house, Lexie had brought Sam into her own big double bed for now, and his nightmares, for the time being, had mercifully ceased. As had her erotic images of Jake in the night...or at least she was better able to curb them.

Since the funeral there had been more than enough to keep her occupied. With Jake's help she had prepared her house for sale and tidied up the garden, mowing the extensive lawns and pruning untidy shrubs, all of which had been rather neglected of late, Dominic having lost his earlier interest in the garden, as he'd lost interest in most things. Since the ads had gone out and the FOR SALE sign had gone up at the front there had been a steady stream of house-hunters through the place, though as yet no serious offers had come in.

With her catering commitments with Bonnie on hold for the time being, Lexie was able to concentrate on looking for another house—a smaller, more modest home for herself and Sam. She had several estate agents looking in the area she had in mind, and Jake insisted on being with her whenever she went to inspect a house.

Most times they took Sam with them, rather than leaving him with Mary or Bonnie. Lexie wanted to give him as much time as she could with Jake, in the short time they had left.

She felt a cold knot in her stomach each time she thought of Jake leaving again. Sam was coming to trust him more each day, and was even prepared to talk to him now and share his small pleasures with him, even play lively, boyish games with him. Already she detected a bond between the two that had never been there between Sam and Dominic.

It pierced her heart in two, knowing that Jake would be going away again soon. It was going to be hard enough for *her* to accept. But how could she explain Jake's departure from their lives in a way that a four-year-old would understand? Sam would want to know when Jake was coming back—or *if* he was coming back—and what could she tell him? Probably not even Jake himself knew the answer to that one.

He didn't even have a house here any more. He'd sold his family home three years ago, during his brief, traumatic visit, when he'd found her married to Dominic. She just hoped that Sam wouldn't feel that Jake had abandoned him, the way *she'd* always felt unwanted and abandoned by the people she had grown to care for. She didn't want that anguish for her son.

When she looked at them together, she knew in her heart that she was being wise to keep the truth about Sam's birth to herself at this point in time. Quite apart from her qualms that Jake would feel she was pressuring him to stay at home—assuming he even believed her—she had Sam to think of first and foremost, his needs to consider. A father who came and went, with the child never knowing when or if he was likely to show up again, or for how long he'd stay if he did, would hardly give the boy the security and permanence he needed right now.

Better for him to go on knowing he had only his mother, someone who he knew loved him and wanted to be with him all the time. Someone constant, whom he could rely on.

Meanwhile, she was grateful to Jake for the help and support he was giving her, now, when she most needed it. Unfortunately, though, the house-hunting was not going well.

'I had no idea houses in this part of town were so expensive,' she moaned after yet another had proved out of her reach financially. She was finding that either the prices were too high or the properties were disappointing in other ways—in too much need of repair, or lacking a safe play area for Sam, or with a kitchen that was unsuitable for cooking vast quantities of cakes.

'Anything this close to the city and in this general area is expensive,' Jake told her with a wry smile. 'You'll have to be prepared to pay more, Lexie, or else stay in the outer suburbs, where it's cheaper, if you want anything comparable to your house at Baulkham Hills.'

She shook her head. 'You know I'm not looking for anything as big or as grand as that. Or with as much land. I'll just have to look in the less salubrious suburbs, that's all. Just so long as it's still in this general area...and has a big kitchen and somewhere for Sam to play...or maybe a park nearby.'

But still it wasn't easy. Halfway through the second week she was beginning to despair. Nothing she'd seen so far had met her requirements. Either the house, the land or the price was wrong. And she was moving further and further away from the area she'd hoped to live in.

She had one bit of good news, though. A couple had made an offer for her house. It was a trifle below what she was asking, but the agent felt that the buyer—a couple with two school-age children—would go a bit higher if she was prepared to meet them halfway.

Jake wasn't there at the time to consult. He'd dropped her off at home after yet another fruitless day's search for a house, and had gone off somewhere else on his own. He'd done that a few times in the past few days, sometimes in the evening, presumably to deal with business of his own. Or maybe to catch up with old friends or work colleagues. He hadn't said.

It reminded her that he would be leaving again shortly, and her heart plummeted at the thought. But she supposed she ought to feel grateful to him for spending as much time with them as he had. At least she would have those memories to hold onto when he went back to Africa. It was some small solace.

When Jake reappeared at dinnertime, he made a suggestion.

'There's one more place I'd like you to see, Lexie. The agent's going to meet us there in the morning.' There was a gleam in his eye, as if this particular house had excited him in some way.

'Where is it?' she asked, eyeing him sceptically. Jake's ideas of a home for her were rather grander than her own.

'You'll see tomorrow. But it's right in the midst of the area you first said you wanted to be. And it's a little gem.'

She sighed. 'We've looked at houses there. They're far too expensive. Outrageously expensive. Even the most modest ones. How much is it?'

'Within your range, surprisingly. The owner's prepared to bring his original price down dramatically to get a quick sale. He's moving overseas. Money's no object to him, apparently. And he likes the sound of you and Sam. Leave any negotiating to me,' he said firmly.

She didn't hold out much hope, but she agreed to go and see the house in the morning.

The second she laid her eyes on it she fell in love with it. It was a quaint sandstone cottage-style home on a gently sloping piece of land, a street or two back from the harbour. It even had a harbour view—a tiny glimpse at least—from the windows of the living room, which jutted out above the single garage underneath. It wasn't a large place by any means, but it had a huge kitchen which overlooked the pretty terraced garden at the rear. There wasn't much room for Sam to play, but it was adequate, especially when she heard that there was a park and a playground at the end of the street.

She turned to Jake with a sigh, knowing it was too good to be true. 'Forget it.' She lowered her voice so that the agent, who was discreetly waiting on the other side of the room, couldn't hear. 'It must be worth a fortune. It's even got a harbour view! The owner will never lower his price to anywhere near what I could afford. Your idea of my range, Jake, is—'

'If you really like it, Lexie, let me do the negotiating,' Jake insisted. 'Take a good look around first, to make sure it's what you really want.'

'I don't need to see any more. It's perfect. But—'

'Then leave it to me.'

She wandered out into the garden while Jake was talking to the agent. When he came out to join her he was smiling.

'He's going to speak to the owner. He's very optimistic. Let's go home, Lexie, and wait there. He'll ring you later.'

'You do realise, Jake, that I can't afford—'

'I know what you can afford, Lexie. I think you're going to be very surprised. Miracle buys do happen from time to time, if you're lucky enough to be on the spot at the right moment. Trust me, Lexie.' His eyes burned into hers, appealing to her to leave the matter in his hands.

She found herself melting under his gaze, and gulped in a quick, unsteady breath. Jake Thorn was the last man in the world she ought to put her trust in. And yet, somehow, despite the bitter scars that still lay between them, she knew deep in her heart that she could. And that she always *had* been able to trust him. Jake had never lied to her. He'd never promised her anything he couldn't deliver. He'd always been honest and open with her. *She* had been the one who had expected…begged…hoped for more. More than he had been prepared to give.

Oh, Jake… For a second she let her eyes reveal her innermost feelings…her trust, her regrets, her deepest yearnings. *Is it too late to go back to what we once had?*

For a long moment their eyes held, melding together in a way she'd never thought they would again. 'Do I take it that I can go ahead?' Jake asked, his eyelids flickering as he broke eye contact at last.

She nodded. 'If anyone can swing a miracle, you can, Jake,' she said, with a wealth of meaning in her words. Hadn't he already swung a miracle of sorts, with Sam? Drawing him out of the timid shell he'd crawled into? And the very fact that Jake had come back into her life now, when she needed him most, was a miracle of sorts as well.

Just how much of a miracle only time would tell.

The eve of Jake's departure for Africa came all too quickly, with no miracle change in their situation. Not that she'd really expected it. Jake was Jake, and she knew he would never change. His work was his life. Adventuring, taking dangerous risks, was his life. He would be a lesser man, at least in his own eyes, if he ever gave it all up and agreed to settle down to the kind of safe, secure life she had once dreamed of sharing with him…the kind of life that Dominic, a different kind of man, had wanted and had offered her.

'Let me take you out to dinner, Lexie.' Jake's hand touched her arm. Merely a light brush of his fingertips, but it made her whole body tingle with longing. 'Now that you've signed on the dotted line and have a new home— and have sold yours—I reckon we should celebrate. Leave Sam with Mary and spend the evening with me…just the two of us. You could do with a night out. Even a grieving widow,' he murmured, 'needs a night out once in a while.'

She glanced up and met his eye. Was he mocking her again? Was he trying to get her to open up about her relationship with Dominic, to admit to her real feelings for the man she'd married? And maybe admit to her true feelings for *him* too…the man she'd once professed to love with all her heart? She saw a teasing light in the glinting blue depths…but there seemed to be a questioning look there as well.

'I see no reason why I shouldn't go out to dinner with you,' she said, striving for lightness. 'Especially since you helped me find a new home. I'm sure Dominic would have been grateful to you, Jake, for what you've done for Sam and me,' she added deliberately, and heard the brittle note in her voice. 'He would have wanted me to go on with my life. Dominic only ever wanted what was best for me. For us,' she amended.

'Did he Lexie?' Jake asked softly, his hand coming up to touch her cheek. 'And yet he didn't seem to make either of you happy. Or himself.'

She let her dark eyelashes flutter down, shivering under his touch. And sighed. Jake would be leaving tomorrow. Maybe it was time she *was* honest about her feelings…before it was too late. Before Jake left her again, and decided never to come back.

'It's never easy, Jake,' she began tentatively, still not looking at him, 'when someone loves a person more than…more than they love them. As—as Dominic did with me.' *As I did with you, Jake…as I still do.* 'But he insisted that I—that what I felt for him would be enough, that a marriage between us would work out because—because we both wanted the same things.'

'And you accepted what he was offering.' Jake's voice was suddenly harsh. 'Love was never as important to you as a home, family, security. Roots. I was a fool to ever think it was.'

'Jake, it wasn't like that!' Her lashes flicked up again, her dark eyes appealing to him. 'I—I felt so lost and hurt and—and desolate when you left me. You didn't seem to care about…about *us*…about you and me. You didn't even seem to care if—if you died in your attempt to tame the Amazon, just as long as you proved something to yourself, and the world. Even when we—'

She bit the rest off, sucking in her breath. She didn't want to talk about the time they'd made love…the only time.

She said instead, 'You left without even telling me you loved me, Jake. You *wanted* me, yes. But you didn't love me. Not the way I—I needed to be loved. I—I felt you'd washed your hands of me, that I had no hope left of a— of a future with you. Ever. Certainly not the kind of future I wanted, dreamed about. And Dominic said that—that even if you did come back it wouldn't be for long…and that you would never want to take me with you on future assignments, as you'd half promised you would one day— not even if I became the best journalist in the world. Let alone ever want to settle down to the kind of life *I* dreamed of having one day.'

'I always knew my cousin was a snake in the grass,' Jake hissed as she paused to draw in a ragged breath.

'Dominic was my only comfort when you left!' she cried hoarsely. Her eyes misted as she remembered that awful time, but the mistiness was more at the memory of finding herself pregnant to Jake—the man she had loved and lost—than at the memory of Dominic's comforting presence.

'I'll bet he gave you comfort,' Jake snarled. 'The minute I was out of sight he couldn't wait to slink in and take my place. Knowing you'd never be more vulnerable, and he'd never have a better chance. And—no doubt—not expecting me to survive the crazy stunt I was attempting. Hoping I wouldn't.'

'Jake, Dominic would never have wished any harm to come to you!' *Wouldn't he?* She wasn't so sure. 'He—he was being realistic, as well as kind, Jake. He knew you'd never want to—to settle down and give me the kind of life he knew I'd always longed for. A home, a family of my very own. He said he wanted the same things, that he'd be a loving husband to me, and a good father when—when the time came,' she added hastily.

She forced herself to meet Jake's eye, forced herself to drag out more. As much as she dared. 'He said that—that he loved me more than you ever would. That *he* would always be willing to give, while you—you would always want to take. As you took *me*, Jake—willing as I was—before you went off to risk your neck on the Amazon! And you haven't changed, Jake. You've been a wanderer, an adventurer, a one-man show ever since! Dicing with death ever since!'

Jake swore softly. 'Is that why you leapt straight from

my arms into Dominic's? Because you thought he'd give you more *love* than I would? More of *himself* than I would?' The stinging questions slashed out.

She gave a muffled cry of pain. It was the same resentful, scathing tone he'd used three years ago, when he'd come back from the Amazon after two long years away, *burningly* eager, he'd bitterly confessed to her, to see her again, to hold her again. Only to find her married to his cousin, and the mother of a fourteen-month-old baby.

It had been painfully difficult having to lie to Jake at the time, having to convince him that Sam wasn't his child. But because Sam had arrived almost a month late, nearly ten months after Jake had left Australia, they'd managed to fool him, as they'd fooled their own family and friends.

She could hardly blame Jake for his bitter contempt at the time. Or now. How could he believe anything other than that she'd flung herself straight into Dominic's waiting arms the moment he'd left the country? She'd had no defence then, and she had none now. Not unless she told Jake the truth about Sam. And to tell him now, the night before he was due to go back to Africa...

No! She couldn't. He would think she was attempting to do what she'd tried to do five years ago. To keep him at home. To tie him down. Only by using his *son* this time she would be giving him virtually no choice. He would feel morally bound to do the right thing. To stay at home with his son. Or at least to finish his current African assignment and *then* come back home. For good.

'Uncle Jake!' A small figure hurled himself at Jake's long legs. 'You're back! You said we could play hide-and-seek when you got home.'

Lexie met Jake's eyes briefly as he swung Sam up in his arms.

'I'll tell Mary we're going out to dinner,' she said hastily, before he could change his mind about taking her out.

At least, she thought, despite the bitter pain of the past they'd managed to become friends again, she and Jake, in these past two weeks. They'd managed to recapture the close bond they'd once shared. And that made her happy. Well…happy enough. At least for now.

But she longed for a closer bond, for more than just friendship from Jake—even if he couldn't give her all the other things she might ideally want from him. She longed for the intimacy they'd once shared. And now that she was free again, now that the pain of the past was largely behind them…

Whatever deep scars still lingered, Jake did still have some feelings for her; she was sure of it. Whether or not they would ever have a future together, the kind of future she longed for—and with him leaving for Africa tomorrow and heaven knew where after that it didn't look hopeful— there was no denying that there was *something* still there between them. Whenever they were together, even with Sam or Mary close by, there was an aching awareness, a simmering tension, an undercurrent of throbbing sexual excitement.

But whatever Jake felt for her he was being careful not to put it into words or actions. Whether he was respecting her period of mourning, or holding back for some other, more daunting reason, she couldn't be sure. Perhaps he was afraid that any small move he made, any admission of deeper feelings, might give her false hopes, unreal expectations.

She gave a deep sigh. Or was it simply that her own feelings for Jake were so intense, her awareness of him so acute, that she was imagining a response in him that wasn't there? Fooling herself that his feelings matched hers?

CHAPTER SEVEN

IT WAS late in the evening when Lexie and Jake arrived home from their intimate dinner-for-two in town.

'Jake, I had a lovely evening.' She thanked him warmly, her eyes glowing like highly polished ebony in the soft light of the lamp that Mary had left on for them. The rest of the house was dark and silent. Mary had obviously gone to bed, as they'd told her to do before they'd left, and there wasn't a sound from the big double bed where Sam still slept each night.

As Jake's eyes met hers she confessed to him softly, 'It was wonderful to be able to have a quiet dinner to-gether...just the two of us.'

There had been no jarring notes, no bitter words, no emotional clashes, nothing to spoil their last hours to-gether. It was as if both had been determined from the start to make it an evening to look back on with tender, pleasant memories.

Selective memories, in her case. Already she could barely remember anything about the dinner itself...the spe-cial delicacies they'd eaten, the names of the fine wines they'd chosen, the details of their elegant surroundings, or even what they'd talked about—except that they'd avoided anything too personal, anything touching too closely on their emotions or likely to spark a sour note or revive hurt-ful memories.

What she *would* remember was every detail of Jake's face, every furrow, every vein, every toughly chiselled fea-ture. Throughout dinner her eyes had avidly traced his sensual mouth, his firm cleft chin, the intriguing line of his bent nose, and drunk in the rough texture of his deeply tanned skin, the tiny flecks of light in the piercing blue of his eyes, the way his brown hair tumbled over his brow and curled round his ears.

She looked into his eyes now, and with a rush of panic she knew that she couldn't let him go like this, without a word, without a sign, without some hint of the way she felt about him, regardless of how he might feel about her, regardless of when, or if, he ever intended to come back.

'Jake, it's been so wonderful having you home!' she burst out. 'I wish—' She bit down hard on her lip as she sensed him stiffen and realised she'd almost said too much, almost blurted out that she wished he could be here with them all the time. Never again would she beg for what he wasn't prepared to give; never again would she put that kind of pressure on him.

'I'm going to miss you, Jake,' she said instead, her voice a breathy whisper.

He lifted an eyebrow. 'Is it me you'll miss, Lexie…or having a man around? Having a willing father figure for your son, a cosy little family unit back in your life?' His tone was dry, his face as inscrutable as the wall behind him. 'You must miss all that now that Dominic's gone.'

'Jake, no!' She raised hurt eyes to his. 'I'm going to miss *you*. You know how I—how I've always felt about you, Jake.' It was a bleak statement, not a plea. She had to let him know that she still cared for him. She might never get another chance.

'Do I?' Jake looked down at her, his eyelids flickering, so that all she could see of his eyes was a burning sliver of colour under the thick lashes. They were standing very close, but he made no move to reach out to her, no attempt to touch her. 'I know what you've always wanted me to *be*, Lexie. And when I couldn't be what you wanted, or *give* you what you wanted, you found someone who could.

'And now you've lost him. You're on your own again, with a young son to support, a home and a family to re-build. If you've been hoping that I'll step into Dominic's vacant shoes…' He paused, watching her narrowly, a sardonic half-smile on his lips.

'Jake, I'm not looking for a replacement for Dominic!' she cried, her dark eyes wide, feverish with emotion. 'I want *you*.' The truth spilt out. 'I've always wanted you. I—I never wanted anyone else!' Realising in dismay that she was coming perilously close to doing what she'd vowed never to do again, to pleading with him to stay with her, to give up his footloose life and settle down, she crushed her hand to her lips and swung away from him.

A bronzed hand shot out and clamped around her wrist. As he jerked her round to face him, her startled eyes leapt to his. She felt a tingling shiver at the dark emotions she saw chasing across his face, even though she wasn't sure what they were, or what they meant.

'What's more important to you, Lexie?' Jake asked roughly. She could feel his breath on her face, but their bodies still weren't touching. 'The secure home and family life you've always wanted? Or the man you say you've always wanted?'

She shook her head, pained by his question, by his expecting her to make a choice. 'Don't mock the things I've always wanted, Jake,' she whispered tremulously, 'just because they mean nothing to you. You know what security and—and roots mean to me. What a stable family life for Sam *has* to mean to me. I…' She hesitated, then made a quick decision. 'All right, I made a mistake rushing into marriage with a—with a man I didn't love…or didn't love enough. But it hasn't put me off marriage, Jake…or family life…with the *right* man.'

She met his slanting gaze bravely, wanting to be frank with him, without pleading for what he couldn't give. Wanting him to know that she no longer expected the impossible. 'Too bad the right man…for me…is an incurable adventurer. A globe-trotting nomad who loves to dice with danger and death.' She spoke lightly, a resigned note in her voice, trying to show him she was learning to accept it, to be realistic.

As her words curled into the silence that followed, she felt a tightness in her throat, wondering if, even now, she'd said too much. She didn't want to drive him out of her life altogether, to lose him for good. Even an occasional visit would be better than none at all.

Jake eventually broke the brittle silence, to say softly, 'To my way of thinking, that makes him the *wrong* man, doesn't it? If he can't be what you want? Maybe you've yet to find the right man?'

Lexie felt herself tense as the question hung in the air. 'I've made one mistake, Jake,' she said slowly. 'I don't intend to make another. I can provide a stable, secure home for Sam on my own. I'm not as young and helpless as I was five years ago.'

'You're saying you're prepared to go on…without a man in your life?' There was scepticism, an edge of cynicism in the softly drawled enquiry.

A painful knot twisted inside her. Going on, without Jake, would be hard, painfully hard. She could feel her heart splintering already. Her having had him here with her for these past two weeks, sharing so much of their time together, the two of them and Sam—something she'd never dreamed would ever happen—was going to make his going away again even more difficult to bear. They'd drawn close again in so many ways—bitter and remote and cynical though Jake still remained in others. If only he could have stayed longer...

But wishing for the moon, where Jake was concerned, could only lead to heartache and misery. Best to cling to what they had, to the close friendship they'd managed to regain. And hope he would come back again...soon.

Jake didn't wait for an answer. 'Mind if I use your phone?' He released her abruptly. 'I want to book a taxi to take me to the airport in the morning.'

'No need to do that,' she said quickly, her heart dipping, settling like lead inside her. Was he intending to go without even kissing her goodbye? Didn't he care for her even that much? 'I'll drive you, Jake. Sam will want to come too, and see you off.'

He shook his head. 'I said goodbye to Sam before we went out. I'll be leaving at five in the morning. I've an early morning flight. I'd rather say goodbye to you now, Lexie, and slip off in the morning before any of you are up. I detest last-minute farewells.'

She almost shot back that he must be used to farewells by now. Maybe he meant *tearful* farewells. And last-minute pleas? She squirmed inwardly at the memory of her futile last-minute pleas five years ago.

'As you wish,' she said, struggling to hide the bitter disappointment welling up inside her. 'Any idea how long you'll be in Africa?'

'Another couple of months, give or take. You should be in your new house by the time I come back.' He paused, pursing his lips as he saw her eyes light up at the words 'come back'. 'As soon as I finish my current series of assignments,' he spelt out, his own eyes glinting above hers, 'I'll be coming back to Australia. For a bit longer next time. I'll see you both then.'

As her spirits soared, she caught back the question on her lips. However long it was for next time, it wouldn't be long enough…not for her, or, she suspected, for Sam either. But it would be something. More than something. And only another couple of months to wait.

'It will be great to see you again, Jake.' She felt tears threatening and turned quickly away. 'I'll book your taxi for you. Five, you said?' She was already picking up the phone, her hand not quite steady.

'Five,' she heard him softly affirm from across the room.

When she hung up a moment later, she half expected him to be gone. Until strong hands gripped her shoulders from behind and spun her round. Her quickly caught breath was almost knocked from her body as Jake dragged her hard up against the strongly muscled wall of his chest, his eyes a bright glitter above hers.

'Here's something to remember me by,' he grated softly. As Lexie gulped a quick mouthful of air into her lungs, he took her face in both hands and crushed his mouth down hard on hers, cutting off her air supply all over again.

He waited only long enough to feel the shudder of response in her body, to feel her full lips softening under his, then he wrenched his mouth away. 'Just try not to get married again before I get back!' The words shot out in a husky rasp.

Then he thrust her away from him and strode out of the room.

CHAPTER EIGHT

NINE weeks came and went, with no sign of Jake, and no word from him other than a postcard he'd sent to Sam on his arrival at Zaire Airport, and some photographs which had arrived a few weeks later in a manilla envelope, also addressed to Sam. The colour photographs, taken along the Zaire river, had a brief descriptive note scrawled on the back of each one. There had been nothing else in the envelope. No personal note. No message for her. Typical Jake, she'd thought with a deep sigh. Not even to send his love, as any friend or relative would do.

Did he feel that the photographs were message enough? His way of showing he hadn't forgotten them?

'Uncle Jake sent them for *me*? All the way from Africa?' Sam had squawked when the photographs had come, his dark eyes lighting up in a way she hadn't seen in weeks.

'Yes, darling. Your…uncle Jake is thinking of you, even though he's so far away. Look…he's even sent a snapshot of himself, holding a baby chimpanzee.' She'd reached out unconsciously to stroke it, brushing her fingers over Jake's suntanned face, her throat swelling with a rush of emotion. 'He's very fond of you, you know.'

Had she been wrong, she found herself brooding anew, denying Jake the knowledge that the boy he was so fond of was his son?

'When is he coming back?' Sam had demanded to know.

'When he's finished his work in Africa, Uncle Jake said. Soon, I hope.'

But for how long would he stay? she wondered now with a tremulous sigh. Could she let him go away again without telling him the truth about Sam? But if she did tell him...

Her heart squeezed in an agony of indecision. What good would it do for Sam to know that he had a father who was going to be continually walking out of his life, never knowing when he'd be back? The boy was unsettled enough already. Missing Jake enough already. To find out that his adventuring uncle Jake was actually his *father*...a father who didn't care enough about him to stay at home with him...

And she couldn't *ask* Jake to stay. Or expect him to stay. She'd never use emotional blackmail.

No. She couldn't do it. She couldn't tell either of them. All she could do was give Sam all the love and comfort that she was capable of giving him, and hope that it would be enough.

And hope that it would be enough for her too.

Luckily, she'd been so busy over the past couple of months that she'd had little time to dwell on the nagging ache inside her that Jake's absence had left behind. Her days were so full, and so exhausting, that by the time she fell into bed at night she was too tired to stay awake for long, dreaming of things that could never be.

It wasn't only moving into a new house that had sapped her energy. Or the emotional wrench of leaving Bonnie and Cliff and seeing them try to be so brave and understanding. It was Sam. He had become fractious and difficult since Jake had left, prone to sudden, explosive temper tantrums. Since settling into their new home he'd become even worse.

Lexie felt consumed with guilt, wondering now if she had done the wrong thing in moving Sam away from his old neighbourhood, away from the two people he'd always loved as his grandparents, away from everything familiar to him. She could understand why the boy was lashing out, why he felt the need to let off steam. He'd been repressed for so long, had bottled up his feelings for so long. Sensing Dominic's sullen hostility towards him, the child had hardly dared raise his voice for fear of triggering an explosive reaction.

Lexie sighed heavily. During the tense final months of her husband's life, Bonnie and Cliff had provided a calm haven for Sam. Dominic's death, coming so suddenly and unexpectedly, had come as a jolting shock to the boy...both a shock and a relief. He'd blamed himself, and withdrawn even further, guilt tormenting him by day, vivid nightmares by night.

And then Jake had come into his life...a caring, dynamic, heroic figure, a man Sam could look up to and admire. But just as Sam had been beginning to crawl out of his protective shell and learning to trust again Jake had walked out of his life. And now he must feel he'd lost Bonnie and Cliff as well.

What have I done? Lexie thought in despair. I've not only made a mess of my own life, I've messed up my son's as well. I'm to blame for everything that has ever happened to both of us. I can't blame Dominic...I can't blame Jake...I've brought this all on myself!

What she would have done without Amy Broome, her elderly neighbour, she shuddered to think. A warm-hearted, sprightly widow, Amy had been a lifesaver. Amy's own daughter and grandchildren lived overseas and, since Lexie had settled in next door with Sam, the old lady had showered the boy with grandmotherly warmth and kindness, patiently cajoling him out of his moods, gently soothing his anger, always being there for them both when most needed.

Amy loved taking Sam to the park to play on the swings and slides and loved reading him stories while Lexie was busy cooking or delivering cakes. She also loved coming in to watch over Sam on the evenings Lexie had to eat out at a local restaurant for her weekly dining-out column, which she'd taken over three weeks after moving in.

Amy had flatly refused Lexie's offers of payment, insisting that her husband had left her well-off, and that having Sam's company, and hers, was payment enough. Lexie cooked the odd meal for her in return, and baked small treats. Last week she had insisted on taking Amy and Sam with her to the local pub for dinner—her restaurant of the week.

Keen for Sam to mix with other children, Lexie had booked him into a reliable day-care centre for two afternoons a week, planning to extend the hours when Sam became more used to it. At first he'd clung to her and hadn't wanted her to leave him, but the carers at the centre had assured her that he seemed happy enough once she was out of sight. Lexie wasn't so sure. Sam was always so relieved to see her when she came to pick him up and, once home, he became more cranky and rebellious than ever. She'd barely been able to draw a smile from him since leaving Baulkham Hills.

Only Bonnie's occasional phone calls, and the few brief weekend visits that Bonnie and Cliff had made together, had perked the boy up. And the arrival of Jake's postcard from Zaire, and later his photographs.

Yesterday, she'd walked into Sam's bedroom and found him gazing at the photograph of Jake holding the baby chimpanzee. His small fingers had been gripping it tightly. The edges of the photograph had become crumpled from what was obviously constant handling. Lexie's heart had twisted at the yearning sadness she'd seen in his eyes.

'You miss your uncle Jake, don't you, pet?' she'd sympathised with a heavy heart. Sam wasn't the only one. Damn Jake! Blowing in and out of people's lives, making his presence felt in the brief time he could spare from the wandering life he loved, and then waltzing off again, sparing little thought for the ones he left behind.

But that was Jake. She'd always known what he was like. And she loved him, despite knowing it. She'd always loved him and she always would. And Sam, for some reason, loved him in the same instinctive, irrational way. And was suffering from it, just as she was.

The strain on her—the busy days and equally tiring evenings, Sam's crankiness, the pressure of trying to give her son a stable, happy home life as a single parent, and her nagging uncertainty about Jake—was beginning to tell. She was feeling tired all the time, emotionally and physically drained. She was losing weight. The face that stared back at her from the mirror looked pale and gaunt, with deeply shadowed eyes, and lips that, like Sam's, had almost forgotten how to smile. Her dark, limpid eyes mirrored the sadness she saw in her son's.

Her life, she realised, was going badly awry. She was making such an effort to prove that she could provide a comfortable, secure home for Sam and make a living on her own that she was failing him instead, failing to devote enough time to making him happy.

She made up her mind to cash in some debentures that Dominic had left her, which she'd been keeping for Sam's future schooling and other expenses. She would cash in just enough to enable her to hire someone to help with the cleaning and other household chores, so that she could spend more time with Sam. It would give her some breathing space to take him out more. To the zoo…to the movies…to visit Bonnie and Cliff at Baulkham Hills for the first time since she and Sam had moved away.

She could tell by Bonnie's phone calls and occasional visits, cheerful as they were, that she and Cliff were missing them both badly. What did it matter if they weren't Sam's real grandparents? With Dominic gone, and Jake gone, who did they have left?

She put the finishing touches to a rich almond torte she was decorating for a special order for the next day and wiped her brow. She felt so tired…so terribly tired. She'd been baking all day, and dozens of log cakes, already cooled and sealed in plastic, were lined up ready for delivery in the morning.

She glanced at her watch. She didn't have to pick Sam up until five. Instead of starting work on her dining-out column, which the local paper needed by tomorrow—she'd invited an old schoolfriend to last night's restaurant—she decided to have a cup of tea and put her feet up for half an hour. The column could wait until tonight. The ironing too.

She carried her mug of tea out into the terraced rear garden and sank into a deep canvas deck-chair. The sun was out and its warm October rays, filtering through the delicate leaves of the silver birch above her, began to seep into her bones. She finished her tea and let her head loll back, her eyes fluttering closed. Within minutes, she was sound asleep.

She dreamed that Jake was kissing her, his lips warm and gently invasive, weaving a sensual magic over hers. Delicious sensations burgeoned inside her. She reached up and curled her arms around his neck, wanting to hold on to him and never let him go. As she felt his kiss deepen, his hungry lips seeking a more intimate possession, her eyes flew wide open.

'What—?' She wrenched her mouth away, her arms sliding from very real shoulders, her eyes focusing on the face above hers. *'Jake!'* Her eyes snapped wider. 'You're back!'

Jake drew back his head, his lip quirking. 'You seem surprised to see me, Lexie. Who did you think you were kissing?'

She shook her head in disbelief. 'I thought I... Oh, Jake, I'm so glad you're back!' In her joy at seeing him, the admission burst out, her dark eyes glowing. 'I...I must have fallen asleep. Oh, heck, what time is it?' She struggled out of the canvas chair, accepting Jake's hand as she struggled to her feet. 'Thank heaven!' she gasped as she glanced at her watch and saw it was only four-twenty. 'I have to pick Sam up at five.'

'Well, what a life,' Jake murmured, peering down into her pale face, his eyes narrowed to sharp blue slits in the bright spring sunlight. 'Must be nice being able to spend your afternoons dozing in the garden while your son is...where is he, by the way? At Bonnie's?'

She felt her lip trembling at the implication that she dozed her afternoons away. Drawing in a deep breath, she told him as steadily as she could manage, 'He's at his day-care centre. He goes there two afternoons a week.'

Something about her tone made him look at her more closely. 'He's enjoying it?'

'He's...beginning to,' she said cautiously. 'He's never really mixed with other children before.' She realised that Jake was still holding her hand, and gently pulled it free, reaching up to brush some silky black strands away from her face. 'The woman in charge assures me he's happy there and is making friends.'

Jake responded with a slight lift of his eyebrow, a comment in itself. 'You didn't answer my question before,' he drawled after a pause, his eyes narrowed again, difficult to read. 'Who did you imagine was kissing you? Or do you kiss any guy who happens to stroll through your sidegate?'

She felt heat flash along her cheekbones, and then drew in her breath. 'I knew it was you, Jake,' she said, deciding then and there to be honest with him from now on...at least about her feelings for him. 'Even though I was half-asleep, I knew it was you.'

'So you haven't taken up with anyone else since I've been away?' He couldn't keep a cynical edge from his voice.

'Hardly,' she almost snapped. What did he think she was? But then...didn't he have good reason to be cynical? She'd been fickle before...in his eyes. Spinning straight from his arms into Dominic's. 'I don't have time for a social life,' she told him tightly. 'I'm a working mother, remember, trying to run a home and make a living. Any spare time I have—which is never enough—I spend with Sam.'

As his brow shot up again, she added defensively, 'I was so damned tired after baking all day, I decided to grab a short break with a cup of tea before starting on something else...and must have fallen asleep in my chair.'

His eyes searched her face, slashes of brilliant blue against the deep golden bronze of his skin. 'Hmm...' he said slowly, bringing his hand up to cup her dimpled chin. 'You do look a bit washed out. You're thinner. Paler. You have smudges under those beautiful eyes. You've been overdoing things, Lexie. No wonder you dropped off to sleep.'

She felt an overwhelming urge to press her cheek into

his warm palm. 'It's been a busy time.' Her tone was still defensive. 'You'll have to excuse the house, Jake. It's a mess.' She'd washed all the bowls and cake-tins, but she'd left them draining on the sink. As for the rest of the house, she'd barely touched it today. She was going to be up late tonight, cleaning and ironing and writing her column.

'Damn it, Lexie, Dominic didn't leave you penniless. Surely you can afford some household help?'

She lifted her chin. 'I intend to...now that we've settled in, more or less. I'm going to get a cleaner in once or twice a week. I want to spend more time with Sam during the day. More...fun time. Even if I have to do more cooking at night, after he's asleep.'

'Life hasn't been much fun lately?' Jake asked softly, reaching out to stroke her cheek with his fingertips.

She felt a spark of resentment, even as she trembled under his touch. 'I've been settling into a new house. Trying to earn a living. Dealing with Sam's—' She clamped her mouth shut. She didn't want Jake, or anyone else, knowing how much trouble she'd been having with Sam. And thinking she couldn't cope.

'With Sam's—what?' Jake asked sharply. 'Nightmares? He's still having them?'

She shook her head, sighing as Jake's hand slid away. 'He's...going through a difficult stage,' she admitted carefully. 'Not surprising, after all he's been through lately. He's just...letting off steam.' She shrugged, trying to make light of it. 'Now that things are settling down a bit and I can give him a bit more of my time he'll soon—'

'Why in hell's name did you want to move so far away from Bonnie and Cliff?' Jake sliced in impatiently. 'They would have helped. And you could have gone on sharing Mary.'

She dropped her gaze under the accusing glare of his.

'I needed to know that I could take care of Sam on my own,' she bit out. 'You of all people should know what being independent means!' She clenched her hands into white-knuckled fists. 'Sam hasn't been neglected. I'm always at home for him. And I have a wonderfully kind neighbour next door, an elderly widow who adores Sam and is as good with him as Mary ever was. She's happy to babysit on the one night a week I have to go out to do my column. I may look as if I'm not coping, but I assure you—'

'OK, OK, hold your horses,' Jake broke in, more gently this time. 'I only said you looked a bit tired. Hey…' He flicked a look at his watch. 'What time did you say you have to pick up Sam?'

'Oh, heck!' She leapt away from him. 'I must fly. Do you want to come with me?' she asked impulsively, pausing for a second.

He beamed at her, the sudden smile bringing laughter lines to his eyes and gentle wrinkles which softened his sun-hardened face, his teeth a brilliant white against his deeply tanned skin.

'My car's out the front,' he offered. 'You can give directions.'

'You've bought a car already?' She threw the question over her shoulder as she darted inside the house for her keys and handbag. How long had he been back? She felt a slight twinge at the thought he might have been back for days, without bothering to get in touch with her until now.

'I have a hire car for the time being.' He was right behind her, his tall frame filling the kitchen doorway. 'I only got back this morning.'

Only this morning… Her spirits lifted. As she ushered him out again, locking the back door behind her, she remembered, 'We'd better take my car. Sam's car seat's in it. I'll drive,' she said, before he could offer.

As they settled into her roomy station wagon—she needed the space to transport her cakes to the specialty shops that sold them—she asked Jake, 'Then you haven't had time to see Bonnie and Cliff yet?' Where did he intend to stay? she wondered, feeling a rush of butterflies at the thought.

'No, but we've spoken on the phone. They suggested coming to dinner on Saturday...the three of us. If you've no other commitments.' He glanced at her as she nosed the station wagon out into the street. 'They tell me you haven't been back to Baulkham Hills since you left.'

She felt heat sweep across her cheeks. It was something she'd been planning to do as soon as she'd organised some extra time for herself.

Her silence made Jake shoot another sharp glance round at her. 'Are the memories back there so bad, Lexie,' he probed with a frown, 'that you can't even bear to go back to see Bonnie and Cliff?'

She felt a tightness in her throat. Wasn't there some truth in what he was saying? Wasn't a part of the reason she'd been keeping away from Baulkham Hills to do with the painful memories going back there would evoke, especially for Sam? The possible effect that it might have on the boy? She had no wish to revive the distressing memories she'd been trying so hard to make him forget...and possibly start up his nightmares all over again.

But now wasn't the time to reveal such things to Jake. He would only probe deeper, want to know more.

'I've been too busy,' she answered tightly. 'Too tired.' But now that Jake was here... Yes, why not go with Jake on Saturday...the three of them together? They could avoid driving past their old home. Sam had always loved visiting Bonnie and Cliff in the past...and with Jake back home again it should be a happy, festive, carefree occasion, so different from the last time he'd come home, for Dominic's funeral.

Sam had still been suffering from shock and guilt and nightmares then, and Bonnie and Cliff had still been in shock too, numbed with grief. To say nothing of the tension between Jake and herself, the bitter scars that his homecoming had exposed, scars that were still there, though, hopefully, not as raw now...

She made up her mind. 'No, I have no commitments on Saturday. It's the one day of the week I don't have to bake cakes for the next day.' Her other chores could wait for once. 'If Sam would like to go, so would I. As long as we're not too late home...for Sam.'

'Bonnie said we could stay the night if you liked,' Jake murmured as she pulled up outside the day-care centre. 'They realise it's a long way for you to come. An hour's drive there and the same back.' His tone was dry, as if he was comparing it with the vast distances he'd travelled in his life. An hour's drive each way would be nothing to a man like Jake.

'I'll see,' she said noncommittally as she opened the car door. There was no sign of Sam or the other children in the fenced playground. 'They'll be inside packing up their things. Want to come in with me?' she asked Jake as she stepped out.

'You go in. I'll wait by the gate.' He waved her on. 'You might want to prepare him.'

'All right. Thanks.' Not that she believed Sam would need too much preparing. Uncle Jake was his hero.

Sam ran to her, the way he always did when she came to collect him. As if he still half expected her not to show up.

'I have a surprise for you,' Lexie said as she hugged him. 'Someone special is waiting outside. Someone you haven't seen since we moved into our new house.'

She felt his small body stiffen, saw his dark eyes flare in quick fear, and cursed her stupidity. Deep down, Sam was still haunted by Dominic's ghost! She was quick to reassure him. 'Your uncle Jake is home again, darling. He's come all the way from Africa to visit us.' She felt a pang as she said the word 'visit'. How long would his visit last this time? Would there ever be a time when he decided to come back and settle down for good?

Sam's tiny face brightened. 'Did he bring the baby chimp with him?'

Lexie laughed. 'I don't think so. Baby chimps like living in jungles, not cities. Come on. Uncle Jake's waiting for you.'

He clung to her hand as they walked out into the yard, as if he still didn't quite believe that his uncle Jake could really be here. But the moment he saw Jake at the gate, the moment his wide black eyes fastened on the familiar bronzed face, a huge smile burst from his lips. He broke away from Lexie and flew straight into Jake's open arms.

Lexie felt a lump swell in her throat as she watched. It was the first time for weeks that Sam had run to anyone other than herself, the first time she'd seen a real smile lighting up his face.

Jake swung the boy up in his powerful arms. 'My, I think you've grown taller while I've been away. You'll be wanting to play cricket with me next.'

Sam giggled. Then he bit his lip, eyeing Jake uncertainly. 'I don't have a cricket bat.' Then inspiration hit him. 'I've got a ball back home.' He turned appealing dark eyes to Jake. 'We could play catchy.'

'Well…that sounds fine to me.' Reaching the car in a

few long strides, Jake lowered Sam to the ground. 'Let's get home, shall we, and have a game? OK?'

'OK, Uncle Jake.' Sam gazed adoringly up at him, his eyes as big as saucers. 'I—' His lip wobbled. 'I'm not very good.'

'You'll soon learn. I'll teach you. That's what uncles are for,' Jake said, ruffling his hair.

Lexie's eyes were misty as she strapped Sam into his car seat. This is what he's missed, she thought, her heart twisting. Having a caring man around. A man to look up to, and learn from, and have fun with. She shivered. Sam had never had fun with Dominic. At least, not since he'd grown from a cute, cuddly toddler into a lively, outgoing little boy—as he'd been before the demons tormenting Dominic had turned him into a timid, withdrawn child.

We both need a man around, she mused pensively as she slipped into the driver's seat beside Jake. Only it would have to be the *right* man next time. For both of them.

She stifled a sigh. There would only ever be one right man for her. And for Sam too, she suspected. She slid a look round at Jake. Now that he was back...was it possible? Would it ever be possible?

Or was she reaching for the moon again?

'Are you back in Australia for long?' she asked, flicking her eyes back to the road in front. She realised she was holding her breath.

'I've taken on an assignment back here.'

Her heart did a double somersault. 'You mean here...in Sydney?' She tried not to show too much reaction. Or hold out too much hope. It was far more likely to be somewhere remote...somewhere out in the raw, challenging outback, or up in the wilds of the far north, among the man-eating crocodiles and the deadly taipans. Jake hadn't spent much time in cities in the past five years. The wilder, the more dangerous the territory, the better he seemed to like it.

'That's right...here in Sydney.' His voice gently mocked her, as if he'd guessed what she was thinking. 'I've been commissioned to do a feature article on Sydney for the overseas market, concentrating on the people here, the human face of the city. There's a worldwide interest in Sydney since it was announced that the 2000 Olympics are to be held here.'

'A bit out of your usual sphere, isn't it? Cities...and city people?' she mocked in return, to cover a fluttery wave of hope. *Why* had he accepted it? Had she and Sam anything to do with it?

'Not necessarily. I've done similar articles in the past. My article on the people of Rwanda won several awards. I like exploring the human face of a place...the human condition...people's emotions: joy, suffering, humour, hope, despair—the whole gamut. People fascinate me. The way they live, what they do for a living, how they relax, how their backgrounds have shaped them, affected their lives...' His lip quirked. 'One day I'm going to be too old and lazy to ride rapids and tramp through jungles. Or I may not want to.'

As he paused, Lexie stifled the flare of hope that had kindled for a second. *One day...* That could mean in the dim, distant future. He was warning her that he wasn't ready to give up his wandering life just yet. She might as well face it. Once he'd completed his assignment here and recharged his batteries, the itch to travel would come back and he'd be off again, seeking a far more challenging, exciting assignment in some dangerously remote part of the world. Adventuring, facing deep perils and challenges, defying the unknown were in Jake's blood.

'Are you going to sleep at our place, Uncle Jake?' Sam asked from the back seat.

As Lexie caught her breath at the totally unexpected question, Jake turned his head and answered the boy with a smile. 'I won't be far away, tiger. Just around the corner in fact.'

'Around the corner?' Lexie heard herself echoing.

'Well, close to it. I've taken an apartment down by the harbour. It belongs to a colleague of mine who's still in Africa. I'll have the place to myself...for as long as I'll be needing it.'

So... Lexie hid a sigh. He had no intention of finding a place of his own. A permanent place. Well, of course not, she thought with a twinge of bitterness. This is Jake. Nowhere is permanent with Jake.

But at least while he was here in Sydney he wouldn't be far away. Was it mere chance that he'd chosen to move into this particular friend's place, a place so near to her own? Conflicting emotions swirled through her: doubt, longing, excitement, despair. Now that Jake was back, how could she face the thought of him going away again? Being without him again?

But he was here with her now, and somehow, already, having him back home had made everything seem right again, brighter, easier. Even Sam had perked up. They both *needed* him.

Not only needed, she thought, vividly aware of Jake's presence at her side, her nostrils flaring at the subtle aftershave on his skin, the scent of his well-worn leather jacket, the very essence of him. She *wanted* him...so badly. *Burned* for him. Her lips still tingled from his lingering kiss this afternoon. Her arms ached to hold him.

'You'll stay for dinner?' she asked him. How much spare time was he going to have while he was here? And how much of his spare time would he be prepared to give her…and to Sam? 'I have some work to do after Sam's in bed,' she remembered, 'but we could have an early meal.'

'I'd like that,' Jake readily accepted. 'Unless you'd prefer to have a rest from cooking? We could always go to a burger place.' He turned his head and winked at Sam.

'Yes, yes!' came a delighted cry from behind. '*Can* we, Mummy?' As Lexie glanced round, her son's big dark eyes pleaded with her. 'Becky's going to McDonald's for her birthday. You never take me, Mummy.'

'I suppose Mummy's been too busy,' Jake said, and Lexie sighed, a guilty warmth heating her cheeks. Sam had never even mentioned McDonald's before. And she'd never thought of it. Yet here was Jake, on his first day back…

'Fine with me,' she said lightly, adding out of the corner of her mouth, so that only Jake could hear, 'I hope you meant it.'

She saw his lips ease into a smile, the old teasing smile she'd missed so much. 'Cross my heart. I've been dreaming for weeks of a nice juicy beefburger and french fries. And today I missed out on lunch.'

'Well…why don't we go now, before the rush starts?' she suggested sweetly. 'Hungry, Sam?' she asked. Sam's appetite was never great, but he was usually hungry after his afternoon at the day-care centre.

'I'm *starving*!' Sam announced, and Lexie's head jerked round, a trill of laughter bubbling from her lips. She'd never heard him use the word before.

'So you can still laugh,' Jake murmured from beside her. 'That's good to see.'

Her smile faltered. Just as she was about to rap back that she hadn't had an awful lot to laugh about lately, she caught the warmth in his eyes and realised that he hadn't meant it in a mocking way, as a taunt. He was genuinely pleased to see that she still *could* laugh.

That was what Sam had missed too, lately, she realised. Laughter. Light-heartedness. Fun.

'It's good to have you back, Jake,' she said, the words popping out. She shrugged. If they revealed too much…well, too bad. It *was* good to have him back. For however long his stay lasted this time.

CHAPTER NINE

ONE good thing had come of Jake's return already. Sam had had no more temper tantrums, no more cranky outbursts. In the past few days he'd thrown all his childish energy into the lively games he played with Jake in the back yard or down at the park, whenever Jake was able to drop in, and into the family outings the three of them had already managed to squeeze into the few days he'd been home. Jake seemed to sense that Sam's needs were uppermost in Lexie's mind right now.

Jake had taken them by ferry to Manly to see the sharks at the Aquarium, and to the zoo to see the animals. He'd spent an entire afternoon with them at the popular Power House Museum, Sam coming away entranced, full of questions about steam engines and space ships, which Jake had patiently answered in minute detail.

Jake was never without his camera on their outings together, and was constantly snapping away—focusing on strangers as much as on Lexie and Sam, often pausing to chat as he took his pictures. Lexie didn't doubt that some of these shots of Sydneysiders at leisure would turn up eventually in his feature article on the 'human face' of Sydney. That, after all, was the reason he was here. This wasn't a holiday for Jake. He hadn't come home for her sake or Sam's. He was on an important assignment for the international market.

So far she and Jake had had no time alone together. He'd come home for dinner a couple of times, but had left soon afterwards, disappearing with his camera to capture

Sydneysiders by night—knowing that she had Sam to bath and put to bed, and cooking and other chores to catch up on. Since Jake had been back she'd been forced to bake late into the night, to make up for the time she'd lost during the day—willingly lost, only too glad to spend whatever time she could with Jake and Sam.

Just being with Jake again for those few hours each day—the three of them together—was pleasure enough, exciting enough for now, sweet torture though it was in other ways. What Jake was doing for Sam meant more to her right now than any needs, any yearnings of her own. Sam was revelling in a taste of real family life—a happy, relaxed, fun-filled family life, with people who genuinely cared for him—for possibly the first time in his young life.

It was ironic really, she thought bemusedly…that Sam should be enjoying family life with Jake, of all people. *How long was it going to last?*

When Saturday came, the day they'd promised to drive to Baulkham Hills to visit Bonnie and Cliff, Jake turned up mid-afternoon to find Lexie and Sam packing overnight bags and a big round plastic cake container into the station wagon.

'You've decided to stay the night? Good, they'll be pleased,' he commented as he greeted Sam with a bear hug.

'Mummy's baked a big cake for Nana and Grandpa,' Sam announced proudly. 'I helped her.'

'And licked the bowl clean after you'd iced the cake, I bet,' Jake teased. He dug his hand into the camera bag slung over his shoulder. 'I found something among my things this morning, tiger, that I thought you might like to have.' As Sam's face lit up, he pulled out a glossy-covered magazine.

He flicked it open to a page of photographs. 'It's an

article I had published earlier this year on the African elephant. There's a picture of two bull elephants fighting, and some young elephants frolicking in a river stream. See their big round ears flapping? And there's one of me with my Pygmy guide…I took it myself, using a tripod.'

As he held out the open magazine to Sam, Lexie drew in her breath, the pictures he'd described triggering a discomfiting memory. She glanced quickly at Sam as the boy reached out to take it, saw his big dark eyes focus on the picture of Jake with his Pygmy guide.

The boy froze, and snatched back his hand.

'It's OK, tiger,' Jake coaxed with a quick smile. 'You can take it. I'm giving it to you.'

'Don't want it!' Sam mumbled, his eyes sliding away. He curled his small hands into tight little balls and backed away.

'You don't?' Jake frowned. 'Something about it bothers you? The elephants fighting…is that it?'

Lexie stepped in hastily, sliding her hands over Sam's shoulders. 'It's all right, pet,' she said gently. 'You can take it. Uncle Jake's giving it to you. It's yours.'

She could understand Sam's reaction only too well. Bonnie had given the boy a copy of this very same magazine a few months ago, after Sam had shown an interest in Jake's article. Bonnie's kindly gesture had rebounded on the child later, and it was plain he hadn't forgotten the ugly incident. But how could she explain to Jake what had happened without…?

'You heard what Uncle Jake said, pet. It's yours to keep. It's OK, you can take it, darling.'

She felt Sam shudder under her hands. 'Don't want it!' He screwed up his face, as if anxious to blot it out of his mind.

'You keep it safe for him, Jake.' Lexie met Jake's speculative blue eyes with an imperceptible shake of her head. 'He feels it belongs to you,' she said by way of explanation. 'Maybe he'll change his mind later.'

'I won't!'

'It's OK, tiger. No sweat.' Jake drew his hand back. 'I'll put it away in my camera bag. See? It's gone. But it's yours whenever you want it. Ready to go to Nana's now? I'll buckle you in.'

'All right, Uncle Jake,' Sam said, brightening. He seemed relieved that Jake hadn't taken offence, or tried to force the magazine on him.

'Off we go, then,' Lexie said, breathing more freely herself now that the difficult moment had passed. She tossed Jake a rueful grin as they drove off. Let him think it was just a small boy's reluctance to take something that didn't belong to him. Or a childish whim.

Bonnie and Cliff greeted the three of them with open arms, delighted to see them. While Cliff was having a private word with Jake and Sam, Bonnie took Lexie aside and linked an arm through hers.

'We've missed you, dear, so much,' she said warmly. 'You were a daughter to us, remember, for many happy years before you married our son. Even if you'd married someone else, or if you marry again in the future, you'll always be our much loved daughter, dear…and little Sam our beloved grandson.'

Lexie swallowed hard. Did Bonnie think she'd moved away from them because she wasn't their real daughter? Could she have sensed that there'd been something not quite right between Dominic and herself? Bonnie seemed to be telling her that it didn't matter, that the links between them were still strong and lasting, regardless.

She smiled at the older woman, feeling warmed and reassured by her loving words. Bonnie was also reminding her that she and Sam were all that the two of them, she and Cliff, had now, and that wherever she was, and whatever she chose to do with her life—even if she met and married someone else—they would still want her in their lives. And Sam, of course.

She felt a wave of guilt. 'Bonnie, I'm sorry we haven't been back to see you before this—' she began, but Bonnie hushed her.

'We know how busy you've been, dear. You needed time to settle in, and get Sam used to his new surroundings. I just wanted you to know, Lexie...we'll always be here for you, Cliff and I.'

When Jake went away again, did she mean? Was Bonnie afraid, seeing her with Jake again and the two of them back on friendly terms, that she was going to end up being hurt, being left in the lurch again? Bonnie had always known how she'd felt about Jake in the past, before he'd gone off to the Amazon, and must have looked on her hasty wedding to Dominic as marriage on the rebound, a desperate attempt on her part to blot Jake from her mind, from her *life*.

Seeing her with Jake now, seeing them so friendly again, Bonnie must be wondering if those old feelings, the passion that had once been there, had flared to life again.

Perhaps Bonnie even had doubts about Sam's... paternity? Maybe she always had?

Lexie pondered on the possibility for a moment, her cheeks burning at the thought. Bonnie certainly must have had her doubts at one time, despite Dominic's assurances, and her own, that the baby she was expecting was Dominic's. Sam's fortuitous late arrival by almost a full month must have allayed Bonnie's suspicions, though... surely? As far as Bonnie and Cliff and their friends were concerned, Sam had arrived on time.

Bonnie couldn't possibly have guessed the truth…could she? Certainly Dominic would never have told her, would never even have hinted at it! And the only other person who knew the truth, their family doctor, had been bound to secrecy. Dominic had made sure of that.

Later, as she and Bonnie were watching Cliff and Jake playing a makeshift game of cricket with Sam in the back yard, Bonnie remarked wistfully, 'Jake's good with Sam, isn't he? And Sam seems to adore Jake.'

Lexie's heart shifted uncomfortably. Was Bonnie remembering how Sam had been with Dominic? So quiet and timid and withdrawn? There had been none of this wild exuberance, this easy camaraderie, this spontaneous laughter.

'Yes…he's very fond of his uncle Jake. They do get on well. Jake's been a—a tower of support since he's been back.'

'Yes…Sam's really come out of his shell,' Bonnie agreed. 'He was so timid and shy before, he hardly opened his mouth. It was hard to coax a smile from him, let alone a full-bodied belly laugh. I suppose—' she seemed to hesitate '—I suppose Dominic's dark moods this past year wouldn't have helped, poor little mite. He's such a sensitive child. You had a difficult time with my son, Lexie, dear, before he…' She trailed off with a shiver. 'I wish I could have done something…helped in some way.'

'Dominic wasn't himself,' Lexie said quickly. Was Bonnie hoping she'd open up, now that some time had passed, and tell her *why* Dominic had changed so much, why he'd been so moody and unlike his old sweet-tempered self?

She took a deep breath. 'I think…I think he felt a bit let down because I hadn't been able to give him a—a daughter. Or a s—another son,' she dragged out, wanting to give Bonnie an acceptable reason for her son's black moods in the months leading up to his death. Bonnie never had to know it was Dominic who couldn't have children, even though it was that harsh realisation which had been the last straw to Dominic, plunging him even deeper into despair and paranoia.

Bonnie didn't answer. She was watching Jake and Sam approaching, hand in hand. Sam was laughing up at Jake, his small face aglow, his dark hair rumpled from his game, his big black eyes alight with the thrill of playing cricket with Jake, and having Jake home again. Jake was smiling down at the boy in the way a benevolent father might look at his much loved son. Lexie's heart twisted.

As she flicked a glance round at the older woman beside her, she saw Bonnie's lips part, saw her soft grey eyes narrow, then spring wide, before leaping round to meet hers.

She knows, Lexie thought in quick panic. Seeing Jake and Sam together, so close together, she's seen some likeness, some common mannerism, *something*. Hadn't Bonnie always said there was the look of a Thorn about Sam, despite the black hair and dark eyes and dimpled chin he'd inherited from his mother?

It was just as Dominic had always feared…that someone would notice the likeness one day and put two and two together. And now Bonnie had. She *knew*.

Lexie's hand fluttered to her throat. Maybe if Dominic had still been here, Bonnie would have shrugged it off, closed her mind to it, put it down to a family likeness. After all, cousins often did look alike. But Dominic wasn't here…and never would be again…and Bonnie knew better than anyone how Lexie had once felt about Jake. And maybe still did…

She gulped as a lump gathered in her throat. Now

Bonnie would realise what had really been niggling at Dominic...what had been making him so touchy and irritable...why he'd appeared to have lost interest in life. Because he'd been bringing up another man's child as his own, and had been afraid that people would find out, or guess...

As she met Bonnie's eyes Lexie appealed to her with her own. *Please, Bonnie, don't say anything...Jake doesn't know.*

The grey eyes, instead of rejecting her unspoken plea, softened. Understanding flashed between them. Bonnie reached out and touched her arm. 'Let's go in, shall we,' she said gently, 'and help Mary serve up dinner? Our cricketers look as if they have extremely healthy appetites.'

Nothing more was said, even when they were alone for a few minutes in the kitchen, while Mary was fussing around in the dining room. But the bond between Bonnie and herself seemed to strengthen from that moment.

Bonnie didn't hold it against her. She couldn't have been warmer, more loving. There was a new calmness about her. Lexie sensed that a load had been lifted from the older woman's shoulders...having an answer to so much that had puzzled and tormented her. Bonnie would realise now what had been behind her son's secret misery. His fear of the truth about Sam coming out, of being the butt of gossip and derision. And, sad as Bonnie must be about what the deception had ultimately done to her son, she seemed to understand. She didn't blame Lexie.

Lexie felt a huge weight sliding from her own shoulders as well. It was such a relief to know that Bonnie hadn't rejected her, or bitterly turned against her, now that she knew the truth about Sam's birth. Such a relief to know that she wouldn't be deceiving this wonderful woman any more. It felt so good, knowing that Bonnie sympathised and understood, and still wanted her in the family. She had never felt closer to her.

Since he'd been back, Jake had met Amy from next door a few times, and they got on like a house on fire. Until the evening Amy came in to babysit for Lexie and let something slip, quite innocently.

It was Lexie's restaurant-of-the-week night, and she'd invited Jake to go with her. As they were saying goodnight to Sam, Amy remarked, 'I've had a lovely letter from the man who used to own your house, Lexie. Such a nice man. He's living in Canada now.'

Lexie smiled. 'He's liking it there?' She had warm feelings herself towards the previous owner. She'd fallen in love with this quaint, cottage-style home at first sight, but had thought she'd never be able to afford it. His generosity had made it possible.

'Yes, very much. And he's enjoying his new job.'

'I'm glad,' Lexie said warmly. 'He sounded a delightful man. Do you know, Amy, that he drastically lowered his price for this house, just so that I could afford it? He liked the sound of us—Sam and me—the estate agent told me. He was anxious to sell in a hurry and wanted *us* to have his house. I was able to buy it for a song. Well, it was a song for this part of town.'

Amy gave a chuckle. 'Is that what you call it, dear? A *song*? You must have got a fortune for your previous home, dear, that's all I can say.'

'What do you mean?' Lexie asked quickly.

'Well…' Amy seemed a bit hesitant. 'I know what Stephen was asking for his house, and when he sold it he told me he'd got the price he'd asked for. He was really chuffed about it. Selling it so quickly. *He* told me he hadn't had to drop his price at all!'

Lexie looked confused. 'But…he did drop it. Jake acted for me. He beat the price down considerably. Dramatically. I'd never have been able to—'

'The owner would never have revealed the details of our agreement,' Jake cut in. His tone was curt, an irritated furrow in his brow. 'It was a confidential settlement.'

Amy bit her lip. She looked as confused as Lexie. 'Then why would he—?'

'It was confidential,' Jake repeated flatly. 'Lexie, are you coming? You wanted to be there by seven, you said.'

She nodded. Even though tonight was a working dinner, she was looking forward to her evening out with Jake. Just the two of them, alone together for the first time since he'd been back.

'I've left some supper for you, Amy.' She smiled at the old lady, drawing a tentative smile from her in return, and a wary glance at Jake. 'And don't let Sam talk you into more than one bedtime story,' she added.

'Don't rush back, dear,' Amy insisted. 'I'll be watching the late movie. It's one of my old favourites. Be as late as you like.'

'You're an angel, Amy.' Jake's tone was gentler now as he touched the old lady's wrinkled cheek, making her blush. He's back in favour, Lexie thought. At least with Amy…

She said nothing until they were in Jake's car, driving off.

'Jake, I want the truth.' She faced him, frowning. 'Did you put any money into the house I bought?'

Did he hesitate for a second? 'Lexie…you read the contract of sale. The owner was happy with the amount you paid. He would never have signed otherwise. Amy doesn't know what she's—'

'Doesn't she, Jake? It sounded very clear to me. The

owner sold for the price he'd asked for. But I didn't pay it. I paid far, far less. So who paid the difference? You, Jake? You were the one who was acting for me. You were the one who dealt directly with the agent and the owner. There wasn't anyone else. All *I* did was sign the papers, once the final figure was agreed on.'

'Then where's the problem? The owner was happy. You were happy. The agent was happy. Lexie, you got the house you wanted, didn't you? Don't go looking for—'

'I don't want to be obligated to you, Jake.'

'You're not obligated to me.' His voice was curt. 'Just forget it. Even if it were true, there's no way you could prove it.'

'I could demand that the agent tell me.'

'Agents don't divulge confidential information.'

'So you're admitting he does have confidential information that he's been keeping from *me*?'

'Lexie, don't spoil our evening.' He turned to her with a quick smile, trying to coax an answering smile from her. 'This is our first night out together, just the two of us. Let's enjoy it. Working dinner or not, I'd like it to be a special night.'

She sensed warning bells. 'That sounds rather...final.' Her voice sounded husky, and she quickly cleared her throat. 'Have you finished your Sydney assignment, Jake? Is this "special night" a lead-up to another goodbye?'

His eyes flicked back to hers. 'Would you be upset if it was?'

She snapped her gaze away, her face tightening, showing nothing of the painful ache she felt inside. 'When something's inevitable, you have to face it. No point in dwelling on feelings.'

'But you do...have feelings, Lexie. You'd miss me?'

'For goodness' sake, Jake. What do you think? Of course I'll miss you. And Sam will miss you. Satisfied?'

Jake said nothing. It was as if he was waiting for her to say more. Or *expecting* her to say more? Expecting her to—*ask* him to stay?

When she remained stonily silent, he raised his brows. 'I'm glad to hear you'll both miss me, Lexie.' His voice was like soft velvet, caressing her. 'But no, I'm not ready to leave just yet. I haven't finished my assignment here.'

She let her breath out...slowly. Then drew in another sharply, to snap at him, 'You like teasing me, don't you, Jake? Why do you do it? Just to hear me say how much I'll miss you when you go?'

'Lexie...no!' He took a hand off the wheel to reach out to her, his fingers finding hers, closing over them. 'Though—OK, maybe I did want to know what you feel...what it is you really want of me— No, don't say anything.' He cut her off as her lips parted. *Before she could beg him to stay?* 'It's enough for now to know that you'd miss me, that we're friends again. That the past is...past.'

His hand squeezed hers. 'It's good being with you again, Lexie. Being able to spend some time together, you and I. You must be lonely now...on your own.' He didn't put it as a question, but the words hung in the air, demanding an answer.

Pain flickered in her eyes. Did he think that was why she was spending her time with him? Because she was *lonely*? Because she felt the need for a man in her life? A father figure for Sam? A neat little family unit to replace the one she'd lost?

Did Jake still believe, after all this time, that all she wanted of him, all she felt for him, was the need to fill a gap in her life, the gap that Dominic's death had left?

Jake, it's *you* I want, not a crutch to lean on...*I love you,* she longed to tell him. But if she told him she loved him, wanted him, he would think she was trying to coax him into staying, that she expected him to give up the adventurous life he loved, as she'd begged him to do once before...in vain. Hadn't he warned her the last time he'd come home, for Dominic's funeral, not to expect anything of him? 'If you've been hoping that I'll step into Dominic's vacant shoes...'

She sighed. No point hoping he might have changed since then. Jake wasn't the domestic, home-loving type. He never would be. Men like Jake needed their freedom too much. Needed danger and excitement too much. They couldn't settle for long in one place. She'd learned that a long time ago, to her bitter cost. Jake had chosen to risk his neck on the Amazon five years ago rather than staying with her, making a life at home here with her. And he'd been risking his life ever since.

She turned away, looking unseeingly out of the window. It was no use expecting Jake to become something he wasn't. If she was ever foolish enough to try to lure him, or entice him into staying at home permanently, she and Sam would be the ones who would suffer in the long run. He would end up a frustrated man, resenting the ties holding him...resenting *her*. The way Dominic had ended up a frustrated man, resenting the life he'd been so ready and willing to take on.

She shivered. No. She couldn't—wouldn't—ever go through anything like that again. The steadily growing bitterness, the dark moods, the tension, the fear of wondering how far a tormented, frustrated man might go. She would never subject Sam to that kind of stress or anxiety again.

She would rather bring him up alone…even if her heart broke in the process.

Enjoy Jake while you have him, her heart urged. Accept what he's willing to give. It will still be more than you ever had from Dominic. And far more than Sam ever had.

CHAPTER TEN

'Is THIS what you studied so hard for, Lexie?' Jake asked as she scribbled in her notebook at the restaurant table. 'Writing up local restaurants? Cooking cakes for exclusive cake shops?'

She glanced up at him. 'My dining-out column is just a temporary job I'm doing for a friend. As for cooking cakes—' she jutted her chin '—I wanted a job I could do from home. I don't like being away from Sam too long. General catering, like I was doing with Bonnie, involves too many nights out.' Too many for a single mother, working alone, she mused.

He made no comment other than to ask, 'You enjoy what you're doing?'

'Yes, I do enjoy it,' she asserted, rather too forcefully. 'I know my subject—thanks to Bonnie. She taught me all she knows about food and cooking. I feel I can write authoritatively on the subject.' She gave a shrug. 'And cooking cakes isn't as boring as you might think. Often I have a real chance to be creative.'

'There was a time when you wanted to be creative in other ways, Lexie. You wanted to write. To create informative, lively articles that people would want to read. All through school and university, and especially when you won your cadetship with the newspaper, you wanted to be a top-flight journalist—the best. It was all you ever wanted to be.'

So that I could work with you one day, Jake. That's why I wanted to be a journalist. To be with you.

'Youthful dreams,' she said dismissively, reaching for her glass of wine. 'That was a long time ago.'

'You were going to travel all over the world chasing stories, the way I chased photographs,' Jake persisted. 'But instead you tossed a promising career out the window in favour of marriage and motherhood. And *cooking*.'

'I decided that marriage and motherhood meant more to me than a career.' She raised her glass to her lips, pausing to take a sip. And to steady her voice. 'And when Sam came along I wanted to be at home for him. Becoming a partner with Bonnie—being able to do most of our cooking at home, with Mary to help out with Sam—was ideal. And it meant I was able to do something for Bonnie. She's always done so much for me.'

'It seems such a waste of a good brain.' Was it pity or censure in Jake's voice? 'There must be better ways to be creative.'

She tilted her chin. 'I *like* cooking. Anyway, what's so creative about being a journalist? It's just reporting. I'd rather be creative in a more imaginative way. By making *up* stories. Writing fiction.'

'Well, why don't you?'

She sighed. 'If I had the time, and could afford the luxury...'

'You must have had time when Dominic was alive.' His voice roughened. 'You didn't need to make a living then. I take it you didn't work with Bonnie *all* the time, day in and day out?'

'Not all the time, no.' She paused to ask how his roast duckling was, and to make a note of his comments. When she looked up again, she admitted, 'I've jotted down the odd idea from time to time, and made up a few children's stories.' She flushed, and made a further confession. 'Actually, I make up stories for Sam all the time. Those animal photographs from Zimbabwe that you left with him the last time you were here...and the ones you sent from Zaire...Sam likes me to weave stories around the animals. And make up poems.'

'You write poetry too? I never knew that.'

Oh, there's a lot you don't know about me, Jake, she thought. 'They're just simple little poems,' she said with a shrug. 'Descriptive poems. Limericks. Nonsense poems. Sometimes they rhyme, sometimes they don't. Sam's forever producing pictures from magazines or books and asking me to make up stories or poems to go with them. It's become a bit of a game. Not that—' she sighed '—not that I've done it so much lately. I haven't had time.'

'You must let me read them.' Jake's voice, rich and soft now, curled round her. 'You've written them down, I hope?'

She flicked him a look, surprised at his interest. 'Some I have. Others I keep in my head. I remember them because Sam makes me repeat them over and over again. And no,' she said as Jake seemed about to speak. 'Don't ask me to start spouting them now. They wouldn't mean a thing without the pictures.'

Jake said nothing, but the warmth of the smile he gave her made her heart melt. *Oh, Jake, I love you. I want you so much. Can't you feel it? Do you feel anything for me? Anything at all?*

She smiled back at him, trying to keep the deep yearning from her eyes. Since he'd been back, he'd barely touched her, let alone kissed her again the way he had that first day. There'd been little time or opportunity for intimacy, with Sam with them most of the time and their evenings spent apart, or with others present. Tonight was the first time they'd been alone together...completely alone.

Just enjoy the here and now... If you start expecting

more, you'll spoil it, and risk driving him out of your life for good.

They lingered at their table long after she'd finished jotting down all her notes on the food, the decor, the service and the general ambience of this better than average restaurant. It was wonderful not to have to worry about rushing home, as she normally did on her weekly night out. Wonderful to feel like a woman again, feminine and relaxed, rather than a harried working journalist in the company of one of her old school or university friends. Wonderful to be in a special man's company. *Jake's* company. The one man in the world she wanted to be with...whatever the future held in store.

'Ready to go?' Jake asked finally, glancing round. 'I think the staff want to clear away and go home. We're the last ones here.'

'Yes. Sure.' She sighed as she rose. She wanted the night to last. To have Jake to herself for a while longer. As they left the restaurant, she made a suggestion with a thudding heart. 'Why don't you show me your apartment, Jake? You told me you have a magnificent view over the harbour. I'd love to see it.'

She wasn't thinking of the view. She was thinking of being alone with Jake. Thinking how much she wanted him, needed him, *loved* him. There hadn't been a moment in the past five years, since they'd made passionate love on that one and only occasion, that she *hadn't* loved him, much as she'd tried to fool herself that her love for him had turned to hate, had crumbled to bitter ashes.

She loved him, and she wasn't going to let him go away again without showing him how much. Only this time it would be different, and she would make sure that he knew it. This time she would be expecting nothing of him. Asking nothing of him. Just *feeling*...feeling what only

Jake could make her feel. She desperately wanted to have something to cherish and hold onto in the long weeks or months that Jake was away the next time. Until he came back to her again.

If he came back…

Jake's eyes held an enigmatic glint as they walked from the restaurant to his car, the shimmering moonlight masking whatever emotions lay in the shadowed depths.

'What if Amy needs to contact us?' There was a whimsical note in his voice as they drove off. 'We left the number of the restaurant with her, but if we go to my place she won't know where—'

'I brought Dominic's pager with me,' she chipped in, flushing in the darkness. 'I told her to page me if she needed to get on to us and we weren't at the restaurant.'

Jake's brow shot up. 'Well, well, well. The night's getting more interesting by the minute.'

Her heart skipped a beat. He sounded… How did he sound? Almost wary. Sardonic. *Something*. Didn't he want the night to last too? To be alone with her?

She licked her lips to moisten them. 'We'd better not be too long,' she said tentatively, hoping to draw him out, to hear him say that he wanted what she did. 'Or Amy will start…to get ideas.'

'I'm sure Amy has ideas already,' Jake said dryly. 'Since I've been spending so much of my time with you.'

'With *Sam*,' she amended. 'As Sam's…as his adored Uncle Jake.' If only, she caught herself wishing, he *could* be more. If only he *would* stay, and be the father he was in fact. She swallowed a sigh. If she told Jake the truth— that Sam was his son—and he believed her he probably *would* stay. He would feel he had to. But how long would it be before he started to get the travel itch again…to resent being tied down…to resent *her*, and maybe even Sam too, for expecting things of him that he'd never wanted to give in the first place?

'Amy knows you're only back for a short time,' she said evenly, and paused, giving him the chance to deny it. Tell me now, Jake, if it's not true…if you've changed your mind about going away again, she pleaded silently. The decision will have to come from you. I'll never beg you to stay. Not again. I'll never put that kind of pressure on you again. And I'll never use Sam as an inducement.

'She does, does she?' was all Jake said, and her heart sank like a stone. Make the most of the time you have left, urged a desperate little voice from within her. Seize this rare chance to be alone with him…quite alone…and savour every moment.

His apartment was only minutes from the restaurant.

'Well, you do yourself proud,' she commented rather unsteadily as Jake switched on the ceiling spotlights and led her in. It was a strikingly bold, ultra-modern apartment, all stark angles and soaring spaces, with streamlined furniture and stunning sculptures in black metal, dark splashes against the white rugs on the polished floor.

'And what a view!' she exclaimed as the twinkling lights of the harbour caught her eye through the full-length windows. But she was even more aware of a crackling tension in the air, a bristling expectancy, and Jake's presence close behind her.

'The view's even better from the balcony,' Jake said, pulling back the sliding doors and steering her out into the night, his hand lightly on her back, his touch bringing a tingling warmth to her skin through the soft wool of her two-piece suit.

A cool breeze wafted up from the water, cooling her heated cheeks. Above them, a layer of cloud hid the stars, but the brightness of the moon shone through, a diffused silvery glow.

'Oh, look at that!' Lexie cried in delight. A cruise ship, strung with fairy lights, was passing by on its way to the Heads. 'What a fantastic sight!' she breathed huskily, aware of Jake's arm circling her waist, pulling her closer to him.

'Mmm...all we need now is some romantic music,' he murmured, his lips lightly brushing over the glossy smoothness of her hair. He began to hum softly.

Tiny heated shivers riffled through her as she realised the tune was 'As Time Goes By', one of her all-time romantic favourites. She began humming it too, then tilted her face to his.

'Jake, it's been a wonderful evening. Perfect. I know it was basically a working night out, but that only made it more stimulating...being able to discuss the menu with someone who's travelled so widely. It's been a long time since I've had such a lovely evening.' Her eyes told him that he was the one who had made it special.

His eyes were a bright glitter above hers, his face achingly close. 'I enjoyed it too.' He touched her face with his fingertips. 'My beautiful Lexie. You grow more beautiful each time I see you.'

'I thought you said I was looking pale and wan?' she reminded him, trembling at his use of the word 'my'. Did he mean it?

'When I first came back, you did. But you don't any more.' He bent his head and touched her lips briefly with his, once, and then again. 'Mmm...I've missed those soft, pouting lips of yours...so much. You smell so good too, and feel good, if my memory hasn't failed me. Dammit, come here!' With a low growl, he dragged her hard up against him, moulding her body into the muscled firmness of his. Then he kissed her again, a real kiss this time, a savagely demanding kiss, his lips searing hers with the heat of a branding iron.

As the fierce pressure of his mouth forced her lips apart, he plunged his tongue deep inside, sending fiery waves down her rapidly melting body. She moaned softly as he leaned her back in his arms, his hips straining against hers, his thighs tangling with her own.

She could barely breathe. His rampaging lips, the thrusting pressure of his taut muscles against her fevered softness were driving out all thought, all reason, leaving only swirling sensations in their place. This was what she had missed…Jake…being in his arms…spinning to heights she had never reached, never could reach, with any other man.

His mouth left hers at last to drag a moist, impassioned path across her flushed cheek. 'All the time I was in Africa, I dreamed of this,' he breathed into her ear, his lips brushing the lobe in a startlingly intimate caress. 'Holding you again…kissing you…kissing you senseless…feeling what only you can make me feel.'

Her crazily thumping heart soared. 'I've been dreaming of this too,' she gasped, her breath quickening as he proceeded to rain kisses down her jawline, along the slender curve of her throat, into the warm hollow at the base. 'I want you, Jake…*you*…only you. So much,' she choked out, feeling almost dizzy at the thought of him making love to her again after all this time.

It would be so different this time, so much better, so much more meaningful, more mutually satisfying. Because her love for him was different…deeper, richer, more giving, not the selfish, immature, demanding love of five years ago. All she wanted at this moment was his love…and to show him how much she loved him. The future meant little

any more. The past was...past. The present was all that
mattered. The present...here with Jake. Now.

'Do you want me too, Jake?' she whispered breathlessly,
curling her arms round his neck and running hungry fingers through the unruly thickness of his hair. 'Please,
Jake,' she breathed huskily. 'Show me you do...*show* me
how much you've missed me!'

She clutched his head in her hands and pressed her lips
to his, inviting him to respond, expecting him to. And in
that instant she sensed that something had changed. Barely
discernible at first, she could feel it in the stillness of his
lips under hers, in the subtle alteration in his hips, his
hands, his body.

She let her hands flutter to his shoulders, her dazed eyes
widening, seeking his, as he drew back, ever so slowly,
and tilted his head at her.

'Don't think this silken web you're weaving isn't tempt-
ing, Lexie.' His voice was hoarse, not quite steady. 'You
think I don't want you?' His voice roughened. 'That I
haven't always wanted you?' He gripped her arms, his
eyes burning into hers. 'But what is it *you* want, Lexie? Is
it me? Jake Thorn, footloose photographer, knock-about
world traveller? Or are you hoping that in your delectable
arms I'll promise to become whatever you want, change
into whatever you want me to be?'

As her lips parted to protest, he taunted softly, 'You
think, now that I've taken on work back here, and now
that I've proved I still have feelings for you, that I'm ripe
for taming...is that it?'

She felt a squeezing hurt. 'You still don't trust me...do
you, Jake?' Her voice was a ragged whisper. 'You couldn't
be more—'

'Try being honest with me, Lexie.' His voice was a
hoarse rasp. 'You can see that I'm crazy about you...wild

with wanting you…and you're thinking that if you give me a taste of what I'll be missing out on when I go away again I'll change my mind about leaving you and turn into the man you want me to be. That's it, isn't it?'

'No!' Indignation and hurt, mingled with the guilt of the past, stung her. 'Jake, I know I did the wrong thing five years ago, begging you not to go to the Amazon, getting all hysterical about it. Using our—our feelings for each other to try to keep you at home. I was so scared of losing you then, of never seeing you again! I can understand why you can't—can't trust me now. I all but threw myself at you, all but forced you into—into making love to me!'

Jake shook his head. 'Don't blame yourself for my loss of control five years ago, Lexie. In the heat of the moment I'd say we both lost control.' He grimaced—as if regretting his weakness? 'Not to worry, it could have been worse,' he said dryly, with a rueful quirk of his eyebrow. 'You could have been unprotected, and just lying about being on the pill. What better way to clip a man's wings than to get yourself pregnant? At least you didn't go that far. At least…not with me,' he finished with a cynical curl of his lip.

She gave a pained cry. 'I'd never have tried to—to clip your wings that way, Jake,' she said in a small voice. 'Or Dominic's either.'

She felt herself dying inside. She *had* been lying when she'd told him she was on the pill. But not because she'd wanted to 'clip his wings' by deliberately falling pregnant. She hadn't even *thought* of pregnancy until Jake had shown his concern about it after they'd made love. She'd told the lie to reassure him that she was in no danger. Not believing for a moment that she was.

But she could see now that Jake would never believe that she'd lied out of concern for *him*… Not when he found out that he *had* made her pregnant, and that Sam was *his* son, not Dominic's. Particularly after she'd heatedly denied it on his return from the Amazon three years ago. And, worse, with Sam being born almost a month late, she'd even managed to convince him!

A spasm of pain pierced her. When Jake found out that she hadn't been on the pill, as she'd told him, he would assume that she'd deliberately planned to get herself pregnant, hoping to force him back from South America—to force him into giving up his dangerous, roving life. And that only the fact that he'd been out of touch, out of reach by the time she found out she was pregnant had prevented her.

He would accuse her of turning to Dominic because she'd failed to trap *him*. Good old faithful Dominic, who'd long loved her and wanted her, and would love and want her baby too.

But it hadn't been like that. It hadn't!

Her eyes, dark with anguish, clung to Jake's. She'd made a lot of mistakes in her life, but deliberately getting herself pregnant hadn't been one of them. The truth trembled on her lips. The truth about Sam...the truth about Dominic...the truth about how much she'd always loved Jake...and only ever Jake. But to tell him now, after what he'd just said...

How could she? He would think she was trying to *clip his wings* all over again!

'If only I knew what lay behind those soulful black eyes of yours.' Jake's gaze swallowed hers. 'There's something...' His eyes narrowed to piercing slivers of blue. 'Now I wonder...' He drew in his lips.

When he went on his voice was hard. 'When I first saw young Sam three years ago and you told me he was Dominic's son, not mine, you said you'd stopped taking the pill after I left for the Amazon. But did you tell *Dominic* you'd stopped taking it, Lexie, when you turned to him for…consolation?'

As she sucked in a fractured breath, he rasped, 'Or did you let him think you were still on the pill? Was that it, Lexie?' His blue eyes impaled hers like icy razors. 'Did you deliberately get yourself pregnant by Dominic, knowing he would marry you if you did?'

He didn't give her a chance to deny it. 'That's all you really wanted, wasn't it, Lexie?' His biting scorn cut into her. 'A husband. A family. A home of your own. You never wanted a career in journalism. You never wanted to travel the world with me. You only said what you thought I wanted to hear. Hoping to bring me to my knees…so I'd do anything, *be* anything you wanted!'

'Jake, no!'

'No?' His mouth twisted. 'So maybe I *was* your number one favourite while I was around.' He was still holding her, but there was nothing loving or gentle about his grip. 'But having failed to keep me at home—and not expecting me to survive the hare-brained venture I was about to embark on—any husband would do…right? Especially a tame puppy dog who adored you.'

'That's unfair, Jake!' Her voice was a forlorn croak. 'I was devastated when you left. And so afraid for you…of what might happen to you. Without Dominic I—I would have gone to pieces. He—he was so kind to me. And I—I wasn't thinking straight. I felt I'd lost you, that you would never care enough to—' She broke off, shaking her head. 'Dominic offered me something I—I never thought I'd get from you.'

She lifted her chin, trying to hide her misery. 'And I didn't trick Dominic into marrying me by getting myself pregnant. I would have had no need to. He—he loved me. He *wanted* children. As much as I did.'

'OK…I take that back.' Jake's voice was still rough-edged, unrepentant. 'You fell into his arms because you were devastated at losing *me*,' he amended with heavy irony. 'Because I'd left you with no hope for the future—at least, not the kind of future you wanted. So you succumbed to my caring cousin—and found yourself pregnant. Whereupon he immediately offered to marry you.' He gave a short, scathing laugh. 'But would you have married *him*, Lexie…if Dominic hadn't made you pregnant?'

His fingers were digging into her flesh, his eyes burning into her face. 'Would you have waited around for me then? Or was the need for marriage and children greater than your need for me? And for the career you always swore you wanted?'

She shook her head numbly, her eyes black pools of distress. 'Dominic asked me to marry him *before* he made love to me,' she whispered, realising as she said it that she was implying that she hadn't been pregnant at the time.

She shivered. The night air, which had seemed so balmy and seductive a few minutes ago, was now chilling her to the bone.

I've lost him all over again, she thought in despair. When he finds out the truth about Sam, and the lies I've told, it will be the end. He'll never forgive me for what I did. Never.

She sagged in his arms, her eyes bleak. 'Jake—' She broke off as she heard a sharp beeping sound. Her pager!

She felt a brief stab of regret, which turned instantly to a flare of panic.

Only one person would be paging her at this hour. *Amy!*

CHAPTER ELEVEN

'I—I HAVE to ring home,' Lexie whispered a moment later, her eyes leaping to Jake's.

'Let me do it.' Jake pulled a mobile phone from his pocket. 'It's OK, I know the number.'

She hovered close as he dialled, heard him ask, 'What's wrong, Amy?' and felt her heart plummet. When Jake said, 'Right...I'll bring her straight away,' she snatched the phone from him.

'Amy, what's wrong? Is it Sam?'

'Oh, Lexie...' Amy's kindly voice wavered. 'He's burning up with fever. And he's been sick. It's come on so suddenly! He—he's calling for his mummy.'

Lexie's throat constricted. 'You haven't called the doctor?'

'N-no...I thought I should call you first. You know what children are like. They can have a high fever one minute, and it's gone the next. He might just be getting a cold. Or maybe one of the children at his day-care centre has passed on something...measles or—'

'He's been immunised against all those things.' Lexie gulped in a shaky breath as she mentally envisaged far worse possibilities. 'Everything but chicken pox, that is,' she remembered. 'Any sign of spots? A rash?'

'No...but they could be yet to appear. He says his throat hurts. He can barely swallow, poor mite.'

'Is he breathing all right?' Lexie asked anxiously.

'Y-yes. It's the fever I'm worried about.' Amy's voice trembled. 'It's so terribly high. It—it's making him shake.'

141

'How high is it?' Lexie asked in alarm.

'Nearly a hundred and four degrees! I checked with the thermometer. I've been mopping him with a damp cloth, and I've given him some liquid Panadol. But it doesn't seem to be helping. At least, not yet.'

Fear tugged at Lexie. 'Amy, we're leaving now. We'll be home in a few minutes. Tell him—tell him I'm on my way. And thanks, Amy…you're doing the right thing.'

In her haste to leave, she almost tripped over a loose rug, and felt Jake's hand steadying her.

'I should never have left him for so long,' she berated herself as Jake sped her home—keeping a watchful eye out for other traffic as the speedometer approached the speed limit. 'He was a bit quieter than usual all day. And he just picked at his dinner. I—I thought it was because he knew I was going out with you…and that he was just feeling a bit—a bit insecure. Left out.'

'Lexie, now don't start blaming yourself. It's not the first time you've left him.'

'It's the first time you and I have been out together without him,' she reminded him, almost snapping in her anxiety. 'A thing like that can make a child feel—feel unwanted and left out.' She gave a trembling sigh. 'But I should have realised it was more than that, that he was sickening for something. But what?' Her voice broke. 'What if it's something serious? I'll never forgive myself if—'

'Lexie, children get sick very easily and recover just as quickly. It's unlikely to be anything serious,' Jake pointed out reasonably. 'If you start falling apart you'll be of no use to him. If you're still worried after you've seen him, we'll call the doctor right away. Or take him straight to a hospital.'

She gave him a weak smile, grateful for his reassurance.

But she didn't want him getting the idea that she couldn't cope without him, that she'd fall apart on her own. Those days were over. If you're looking for a crutch to lean on, forget it, he'd as good as told her. She certainly didn't want him thinking that was what she wanted of him.

'I'm not going to fall apart,' she said tightly. 'It's only natural I'm worried. No mother likes to hear that her child is sick, and a high fever is always a worry. And not knowing what's causing it...'

She trailed off as she felt his hand closing over hers, its comforting warmth seeping into her skin.

'It could be a lot of things, Lexie. A throat infection, a twenty-four-hour virus...' His hand squeezed hers. 'Let's not start imagining it's something serious. It's come on so suddenly. It could go just as quickly. Children can bounce back in no time.'

'I know,' she conceded, and realised that not so long ago she would have leapt at his throat and demanded to know how a footloose adventurer like himself could possibly know what a sick child was likely to do. But Jake *did* know about children. She'd seen evidence of it, over and over again, with Sam and other children they'd encountered since he'd been back home. He had a natural affinity with children...perhaps *because* of his extensive travels. In these past couple of weeks he'd shown more understanding of children—of *her* child—than Dominic had ever shown, despite his professed love of home and family.

'Thanks for the moral support, Jake,' she added in a softer tone. 'Don't think I don't appreciate it. But—' her anxiety flared anew '—I can't help worrying... imagining...' She bit her lip. 'Sam is all I have. I'm all he has. He relies on me to keep him safe and—and well.

If anything happened to him...' She shuddered, her stomach knotting.

'Yes, I know,' Jake said gently. 'You feel scared. You feel responsible for what's happened...even though whatever's wrong with him is not your fault. You're a mother. He's your only child. A child is an awesome responsibility...especially when you're bringing him up on your own. Not that you're entirely alone, Lexie. You have people to help you. Amy...Bonnie and Cliff...your friends. And I'm here.'

She bit back the words she would have snapped at him once. Oh, yes, you're here now, but for how much longer?

'I can manage,' she mumbled.

She felt faintly chilled as his hand slid away from hers, but it was simply because he needed both hands on the wheel to swing the car round into her driveway. At the same time she heard him mutter something and had to strain her ears to catch the words. They sounded like, 'I do believe you can.'

She had no time to dwell on whether he'd sounded mocking or admiring, leaping from the car almost before it came to a halt.

She nearly cried out when she saw Sam. His big dark eyes were dull and glazed with fever, his cheeks flushed, a marked contrast to the deathly pallor of the rest of his face, his slight body huddled up as if he couldn't get warm. Amy was mopping his brow with a damp cloth, but she drew back her hand and stepped aside as Lexie bent over him.

'Mummy's here, darling,' she whispered, fear gripping her at the sight of him. He looked so unlike the lively, bright-eyed boy he'd been since Jake had come home. When she touched his brow his fevered skin almost sang under her fingertips.

'Mummy.' His lips formed the word, but no sound came out. When she touched his hand she could feel it trembling.

'Don't try to talk, darling,' she whispered. 'Mummy's here with you now.' Her brow creased in a frown. His neck looked swollen and puffy. As she ran her fingers lightly under his jawline, the child moaned. She glanced fearfully up at Jake. 'His glands are up,' she breathed.

'Look, it's probably just some virus that's going around,' Jake said soothingly at her shoulder.

'I just took his temperature again,' Amy said worriedly from behind them. 'It's gone up a bit more, Lexie. The Panadol can't have taken effect yet.'

'He's never had a temperature as high as this, ever.' Lexie's hand was unsteady as she mopped the child's burning brow with the damp cloth Amy had handed to her. 'I'll have to call the doctor. I can't leave it till morning.'

'Let me call him,' Jake offered.

'No...I'd better speak to him myself.' Lexie straightened. 'Will you stay with him, Jake? Amy? Just for a minute?'

'Sure we will. Eh, young fella?' Jake bent over Sam, taking the damp cloth from Lexie and brushing it over the child's face as Lexie darted from the room.

She was back within minutes. 'The doctor's on his way.' She cast an anxious look down at her son, then glanced at Amy. 'Amy, you go home to bed,' she said gently. 'We've kept you up far too late. Thanks for—for being here for Sam. You've been wonderful.'

'He'll be all right, Lexie.' Amy gave her arm a squeeze. 'I'll say goodnight, then...I know he's in good hands now. Just call me if you need anything. Any time of the day or night.'

'Amy...thanks.' Lexie gave her a warm smile as she sank into the chair beside the bed.

'I'll see you home, Amy.' Jake swung after her.

'There's no need.' Amy tried to wave him back. 'I'm only next door.'

'I'll see you to your door,' Jake insisted. 'Back in a minute,' he told Lexie as he followed Amy out.

Lexie let her shoulders slump as they left, feeling suddenly, chillingly alone. She hadn't realised how much Jake's presence had been buoying her up, and how much his calm reassurances had been holding back the fear and despair that threatened to engulf her. If she ever lost Sam...

'Sam...my precious boy,' she whispered, brushing the damp cloth over the child's hot skin. 'Fight it, my darling...whatever it is.' I'm not going to lose you the way I've lost everyone else. I won't! she thought. She choked back a sob, blinking away the hot tears that welled in her eyes.

'Please, God,' she breathed shakily, 'don't let it be anything serious. I love my son more than anything in the world. He's the only one who's ever truly belonged to me; he's a part of me, my own flesh and blood. Please don't take him away from me! I'd give my arms and legs for him...my eyes...my life...'

She lifted her son's limp hand and pressed her lips to his burning skin. *Oh, Sam...if you only knew the joy you've given me from the day you were born. You've given some meaning to my life...a reason for going on. You're the best thing that's ever happened to me.*

She felt a hand on her shoulder and jumped. 'He'll be fine, Lexie. He's a strong, healthy kid.'

She glanced up. Involuntarily, gratefully, her hand came up to cover Jake's. 'Thanks, Jake...for staying with me.' In that moment she didn't care if he saw the yearning in her eyes, the deep love she felt for him, the need... She did need him. Now, tonight, most of all.

'Sounds like the doc's car now.' Before drawing back his hand Jake clasped hers for a second. 'I'll go and let him in.'

Half an hour later the doctor had been and gone.

'Tonsillitis!' Lexie shook her head. 'Sam's never had it before. No wonder his throat's so sore and no wonder his glands are so swollen and painful. Dr Frost says his temperature could stay high for days... It's quite common with tonsillitis.'

'Well, at least you can stop worrying, now that you know what it is.' Jake's warmth and strength enveloped her as they stood together by the bedside. 'And just look at him now...sleeping peacefully at last. That jab in his bottom must be doing something already. Why don't you try to get some sleep yourself?'

She turned her head to look up at him, staring into the tanned, ruggedly handsome face that she loved with all her heart...perhaps never more than at this moment. For all her assertions that she could manage on her own, it felt so good having him here with her now...when she needed him the most.

'I don't think I could sleep just yet,' she said as they both tiptoed from the room. 'It must be reaction.' She raked her hair back from her face, the shining strands a striking black against her pale skin. 'I'd like to just relax for a while...unwind. How about I make some coffee? Will you stay a while longer, Jake?'

Her dark eyes appealed to him, but not in the way they had earlier in the evening, in limpid, seductive invitation. Right now she simply wanted him with her...as a dear, trusted friend rather than a lover. She felt too emotionally drained for anything else. Besides, after the way he'd broken off their lovemaking earlier, to question her motives and thrash out the past, there was little likelihood that he'd try to recapture their former mood again tonight!

As she met Jake's gaze, she saw his eyes shimmer with some indefinable emotion. For a long moment his eyes held hers, probing, searching, their blueness deepening, as she watched, into a tenderness she hadn't been expecting.

'I don't think it's coffee you want, Lexie. It's a relaxing drink. You sit down...I'll see to it. I know just what you need.'

He was right. When she took a sip of the brandy he handed her and felt its fiery heat flame down her throat and spread through her veins, she gave a deep, contented sigh and sank back in her chair, letting her head rest against the cushion behind.

A few more sips and she was feeling very relaxed indeed.

Almost dreamily, she murmured, 'Do you know, Jake, you've never told me exactly how you broke your nose? I only know it happened on your Amazon trip.' When she'd first noticed it, on his bitter return home three years ago, she'd been far too wary and uptight to bother about something as trivial as a broken nose.

'I broke it twice, as a matter of fact.' Jake's smile was rueful. 'I rolled my kayak on a particularly vicious stretch of the upper river and ended up bruised all over. With no one around to help, I was lucky to get out of it.'

She shivered. 'Tell me about it, Jake. You never really have. Not in any depth.' The truth was, she'd never encouraged him to talk about it. The subject had always been fraught with too many bitter memories and cruel reminders of the mistakes she'd made and been forced to live with ever since. She hadn't even read the series of articles Jake had had published not long after his stunning triumph.

With things the way they were at the time, she hadn't wanted to be reminded of him.

Neither, naturally enough, had Dominic. And Bonnie and Cliff, sensing that Jake's brief, unannounced visit home had disturbed both of them, had never shown them Jake's Amazon articles. They hadn't even mentioned their wandering nephew again until months later, after Jake had won some perilous kayak race in China. Since then Bonnie had mentioned him briefly from time to time, when she'd had a call from him or read of his exploits in some magazine or newspaper.

Lexie recalled the magazine Bonnie had given Sam earlier in the year, featuring Jake's article on the African elephant…the same article that Jake had tried to give Sam the other day. But she didn't want to dwell on that now.

'Well, I knew it was going to be no picnic,' Jake admitted with an ironic smile. 'People before me had died in the attempt, and others had tried and failed. A lot of the Amazon area is still unexplored and unmapped. You have to be prepared for anything. Boulder-strewn rapids that toss you about like flotsam. Monster whirlpools. Gigantic rocks that rain down from canyon walls so high you can barely see the top.

'I was sucked into a deep, dark gorge for over a week, and forced to survive on oatmeal and sheer nerve. At night, in that endless gorge, I'd have nightmares of what the next day might bring…while I nearly froze to death!'

Her eyes widened in horror. She'd known it had been tough, dangerous, needing massive strength and courage, but she'd had no idea…! 'And you were on your own? The whole time? What about the land crew who were following you?'

'I didn't see much of them. A hiking party met me at strategic points to resupply me, and a film crew in a Land

Rover popped up from time to time…where they could. And, of course, I met people along the way, even in the remotest parts. The odd fisherman or gold-panner. Indian tribes, who let me stay in their villages. Some of the people I met had never even seen a white man before. One alarming-looking fellow threatened me with a poisoned arrow, but we ended up good mates.'

She shuddered. 'No wonder you refused to take me with you, Jake. Even as part of the land crew.' He'd warned her he would need all his concentration. Now she understood. 'Was it tough going all the way?'

He shrugged, flashing a grin. 'The first six hundred miles were the worst. It was wild. Bruising! The river makes its own rules. You have to accept its power. A lot of the upper river was blocked by landslides, and I'd have to tramp for miles, carrying my kayak. And there were snakes. And piranhas. By contrast, the last few months were easy. I only had to worry about the heat—it was brutal—and some pretty fierce storms.'

Lexie could sense his exhilaration, even now. He'd achieved something he'd always wanted to do…something that many others had tried to do and failed. He'd conquered his Everest. And several other Everests since then. Was he satisfied now?

'Do you still go kayaking, Jake?' she asked, hiding a shudder as she wondered what other mishaps besides a broken nose he'd suffered in the past three years.

'Sure. In my spare time…when I've been lucky enough to have some.'

The spare time he could have used to come home, Lexie thought, but he never had. Until after Dominic's death.

'But I may not be so foolhardy from now on.' Jake leaned back languidly. 'I've run rivers in these past three years that no one's ever conquered before. But at the time

I tackled them I didn't care all that much if I lived or died. Now…' he sought her eye and held it '…maybe I do.'

Her lips parted, her mouth feeling suddenly so dry that she couldn't speak. Or was it that she didn't dare? Didn't dare *hope*?

He plucked her empty glass from her fingers. 'Another brandy?' he asked, still holding her glass.

'No. Thanks.' She swallowed. 'I might sleep too heavily and not hear Sam if he wakes up.'

'Would it help if I stayed the night?' Jake asked softly. 'Between the two of us, one of us should hear him if he wakes. Not that I think he will. The doc seemed to think he'd be out till morning.'

She tried to ignore her quickening heartbeat. 'Would you, Jake?' She heard the yearning note in her voice, and it was like cold water dashing over her. If Jake heard it too… 'You…don't have to,' she added in a small voice. 'I'll be OK.'

'You don't have to keep convincing me that you can manage on your own, Lexie.' The corner of Jake's mouth lifted a trifle. 'I've already seen for myself that you can. You're successfully supporting yourself. You've done wonders with this house, turning it into a home to be proud of. And you're doing a great job with Sam. He's a terrific kid.'

'I…I wasn't doing so well when you first arrived,' Lexie reminded him, honesty plucking the admission from her. Or was it the brandy loosening her tongue? 'Sam was difficult to handle when we first moved here. He was cranky and disobedient. It was reaction, I realised that. It's been a traumatic time for him these past few months. He just needed to let off steam, but it still wasn't easy to cope with. And I was so busy every minute of the day…and always so tired, even with Amy giving a hand with Sam.

I wasn't coping too well at all. Until you came and—and things got back on to a more even keel.'

'You would have got there without me, Lexie,' Jake assured her calmly. 'You'd just moved into a new house. Into a new part of town. Into a new job. It's been a hectic time. Anyone would have been exhausted. Lexie, you've proved to me and to everyone else how capable you are...as a working woman *and* as a mother. Don't be so hard on yourself. You're doing a great job. And now that you're going to get someone in to help around the house...well, that'll take some of the pressure off you.'

She nodded, summoning a smile. But contrarily, rather than feeling consoled, she was aware of a slight pang. He sounded *relieved* that she was capable of managing without him, that she was willing to raise Sam alone. When the time came for him to go away again, he would be able to leave with a clear conscience, knowing that she'd be able to cope perfectly well without him.

But it's not your help and support I need, Jake, she wanted to cry out to him. It's you I want. Just you. Sam and I...we both want you, need you, love you, because of the man you are, not because of what you can do for us.

She tried to get up from her chair and felt the room sway. She might have toppled back but for Jake's supporting hand, shooting out to steady her.

'Sorry. Too much brandy,' she gulped.

'You're exhausted.' Before she knew it, Jake was scooping her up in his arms. 'It's not just the brandy. You're worn out. Emotionally drained, I'd say, more than tired. I'm taking you to bed.'

It felt so good being in his arms. So *right*. She let her head loll onto his chest, breathing in the subtle male scent of him, exulting in his warmth, his strength.

'You're wonderful, Jake,' she heard herself murmuring

aloud. The brandy had definitely loosened her tongue! 'Wherever you go in the world,' she added, slurring her words a little, 'I want you to remember that I think you're wonderful.'

She curled her arms round his neck, snuggling her face into the warmth of his throat. 'And Sam thinks you're wonderful too. Will you remember *us*, Jake, when you're away on the other side of the world? We'll be here...waiting until you come back. We'll always be here for you. I'll never marry again, Jake,' she promised him. 'I won't make that mistake again.'

She felt his body quiver slightly. 'You seem determined to send me to the far reaches of the earth,' he said dryly, a faint huskiness in his voice. 'I'm not ready to leave just yet. And when I do it might not be so far away. I'm thinking of taking on another assignment here in Australia.'

'Oh, Jake...do you mean it?' She raised her head. 'Where?'

'All over the country. An international publisher wants me to do a big Australian book for them. Coffee-table stuff, but something a bit different from the usual glossy landscapes and glamorous images. They want the focus to be on the people—people of all ages and types and cultures. I'll be covering the whole continent—the cities, the country, the coast, the outback. It'll be a long-term project.'

He was warning her that he'd be away for a long time. Spending time—lots of it—in far-off, remote corners of the country. As remote as if he'd gone overseas.

But it wouldn't be darkest Africa. It wouldn't be the untamed Amazon. It wouldn't be some distant, alien country with chilling, unknown dangers. It would be here...in Australia. His home country. *Her* home country. With luck, he would be able to pop home from time to time.

'Since I've been back,' Jake went on as he bore her down the passage to her bedroom, 'I've realised the scope there is here in Australia, the exciting possibilities. I've had lots of experience overseas. I've made an international name for myself. People all over the world look for my work. Now I want to apply my experience to my own country. And show it off to the world.'

He carried her into her bedroom without pausing to switch on the overhead light.

'Stay with me a while, Jake,' she pleaded, sliding her fingers through the tousled softness of his hair. 'Please. No strings,' she promised huskily.

In the glow of the light from the passage, she couldn't read the expression in his eyes. But their sudden glitter caused her bones to melt.

As he lowered her onto her bed, she held him even tighter, clinging to his neck, deliberately pulling him down on top of her. She gasped as his heavy weight and firmly packed muscles pressed down on her quivering softness, his powerful thighs straddling her stockinged legs.

'Oh, Jake!' she breathed, straining her body against his, feeling wonderfully erotic sensations, and wanting to feel more. 'I want you so much. I've wanted you for so long...only you, Jake.'

He groaned against her lips, 'Yes, the time is right now, Lexie...finally it's right.'

She wasn't sure what he meant...didn't care. Her full lips were pliant and yielding under his, her heart beating a wild tattoo against the grinding muscles of his chest, her eager fingers tangling convulsively in his hair.

Heat flooded her as he cupped her breast with possessively demanding fingers, fiery sparks exploding from the deepest recesses of her body. She heard panting, gasping sounds that she realised were coming from her own throat.

Her body heaved, arching against his, shock waves hurtling through her.

'Lexie...my adorable, irresistible Lexie!' Jake groaned as she writhed beneath him, his hot, moist lips searing her cheek, her chin, her throat with ever wilder kisses.

'Jake! Oh, please, Jake!' she panted, an intolerable hunger growing inside her with each fevered kiss. 'You're driving me wild!'

He chuckled softly, and drew back his head. 'I've always been wild for *you*, Lexie...never more than at this moment!' For a second he smiled down at her, a full-lipped, sensual smile that showed his teeth, raw desire in the hot glitter of his eyes.

With her eyes still clinging to his, she began to tear at the buttons of his shirt. Jake gave a soft moan, and caught her wrists. 'Lexie...' His voice seemed to flow over her skin like heated honey. 'Are you sure?'

Sure she knew what she was getting into, he meant. A love affair with no strings, no demands. Taking him just as he was.

'Very sure.' She splayed her fingers across his chest, tentatively feeling its moist smoothness, its fiery heat. She felt him shudder under her touch. Then he was fumbling with her jacket, peeling it away from her shoulders, discarding it.

With a quivering sigh, she wriggled up a little so that he could reach behind to unclasp her lacy bra and throw that aside too. His fingers traced around the soft fullness of her breast, the intimate exploration triggering a hot eruption of desire. Her breathing quickened, her thumping heart keeping pace.

'I'd forgotten how smooth your skin feels under my hands, Lexie.' His own breath was coming in harsh rasps, thickening his words. 'I've missed you. God knows I've missed you!'

He sank his face into the creamy flesh where his stroking fingers had just been, his suckling lips and flicking tongue bringing the sensitive peak to exquisite life, making her die a little from the sheer pleasure of being kissed so intimately by him, after all this time.

At the same time their hands were feverishly at work, ripping off the rest of their clothes piece by piece, until they were both lying naked on the bed, revelling in skin on skin.

Lexie's hands stroked, deliberately slowly, his shoulders, his back, his buttocks, her heart pounding an erratic rhythm with each caress. She wanted to explore every part of him, to find the places that would make him ache with need, the way he was making her ache and arch with his roaming hands and seeking lips.

She let her fingers trail down over his rock-hard thighs...her fingertips circling his knee teasingly, then moving up again, brushing over the crisp hairs and the warmth between his legs.

A spasm shook his body. 'You're setting me on fire, Lexie!' His words were thick, slurred with passion. 'No one but you has ever...can ever...' He stifled the rest by burying his face in the silken hollow between her breasts, cupping his hands round her soft buttocks with possessive need, smothering her against his pulsing body.

He was fast losing control...she could feel it. Through the haze of her own desire, a reluctant memory surfaced. Five years ago they had both lost control...and afterwards, when he'd shown concern for her, she had told him she was on the pill. But she hadn't been...

She went still. She couldn't let him think—

'Jake...I'm not on the pill!' The admission spilt out. She

was never going to conceal anything from him again. There was enough already waiting to be revealed.

'Ah.' With a sigh he rolled away from her, drawing a gasp of dismay from her at his abrupt withdrawal. Didn't he even want to *hold* her any more, not even touch her?

'Just a minute,' he growled. 'Luckily…' He fumbled for the trousers he'd thrown to the end of the bed, and plucked something from his pocket. 'Not that there's any danger from a health point of view. I'm well aware of the dangers of foreign travel. But thanks for telling me… I'd assumed you were on the pill. Best not to take any chances.'

Relief flowed through her. He hadn't been rejecting her, hadn't been turning away from her. He was being responsible. Wanting to protect her. And himself, of course.

'Come here, Lexie.' He pulled her back into his arms, their passion mounting again as if there'd been no interruption, bursting into flame, raging out of control.

Senses swimming, she clasped him to her, her mouth clinging to his, her body writhing, shifting beneath his, guiding him inside her. She felt the muscles in his back bunch and flex with unbearable tension, and gasped as a similar tension wound through her with fierce, electrifying intensity.

She wanted the waves of pleasure to last for ever, and yet she was frantic for them to end, to end in the throbbingly wonderful place he was taking her. 'Jake…oh, Jake, yes! *Yes!*'

Wild urgency took over, blinding them both as he made her completely his own, plunging her entire body into such an ecstasy of blissful magic that she sobbed for joy, tears streaming down her face.

'Oh, Jake, I love you, I love you!' The admission slipped from her lips with soul-wrenching yearning as the ripples convulsing them gradually subsided. 'I've always loved you; I always will!' Euphoria smudged her voice. 'No matter where you go in the world, or how long you stay away, I'll never stop loving you, Jake, never!'

He rolled off her, still holding her in his arms, and lifted his head, his eyes warm, darkly shining in the dimness. 'I believe you really mean it this time, Lexie.' His lips, still moist from the turbulence of their kisses, curved into a tender smile. 'I believe you love me now the way I always hoped you would. Unconditionally.'

Without strings, he meant. An unselfish, undemanding love. Yes, her love had changed…matured…deepened.

'Mmm…' she murmured, but deep down inside her heart dipped a little. He had what he wanted now. He could go on his way, knowing that she loved him and would wait for him until the next time. Knowing he had her total, unconditional love.

'I love you too, Lexie.' He lowered his head and kissed her on the lips. 'I always have. I always will.' Her world spun. 'You…do? Why—why didn't you ever tell me?' Because previously she would have expected too much of him? And now he knew that she didn't? That she wasn't going to demand anything more of him, demand the impossible, beg for what he wasn't willing to give?

'The time wasn't right,' he said briefly. 'Now it is. Lexie, I—' He broke off, his head jerking round. 'Did you hear something?'

'Sam?' She was off the bed in a flash, snatching up her dressing gown from the back of a chair as Jake grabbed his trousers and hastily pulled them on.

She ran ahead of him into Sam's room. The child had stirred and rolled over, but he was still fast asleep, even snoring a little.

She felt his brow. 'He feels OK,' she whispered, covering him and tucking him in more securely. 'Look at him…he's sleeping like a baby.' She reached for Jake's hand and pulled him from the room. 'I guess we'd better try to get some sleep ourselves.'

His arm slid round her waist. It was a comforting gesture this time, not a provocative one. 'He'll bounce back in no time now, Lexie. You'll see. And yes…you must get your sleep. I'll just grab my things and—'

'You're not going, Jake?' Her eyes leapt to his, dismayed at the thought of him leaving, tonight of all nights. 'Wouldn't you like to be here if…when Sam wakes up?' She smiled up into the tough, sun-bronzed face she loved. 'It will brighten him up, knowing you're here.'

'Well…sure. OK.'

She tugged him across the passage to her bedroom. 'Sleep in here, Jake…with me. There's plenty of room.' She waved to the queen-sized bed, blushing at the rumpled duvet.

Jake gave a wry grin and shook his head. 'You won't get any sleep if I'm in here with you. And you need it. I'll bunk down in the spare room. Get your sleep, Lexie, for what's left of the night. Sam will be just fine by morning, you'll see.' He squeezed her hand. 'He's a great kid.'

Her eyes misted. 'Sam thinks a lot of you too, Jake. He looks up to you…more than anyone else. He…loves you, I think.'

Jake's eyes met hers. 'I love him too, Lexie. I love him as much as if he were my own son.'

Her heart stopped. 'Oh, Jake.' Her body trembled. She couldn't hold it back any longer. She had to tell him…regardless of the consequences. He had to know.

'Jake…' She clutched his hand. 'Sam…he *is*your son!'

CHAPTER TWELVE

JAKE froze. Only his lips moved as he pulled them back from his teeth to demand harshly, 'What the hell are you playing at now, Lexie? You think now that Dominic's dead and not here to dispute it—'

'No, Jake!' Her fingers trembled on his arm. 'It's the truth! And Dominic knew it…right from the start. He was the only one who ever knew!' Except for Bonnie, who'd guessed the other day. But that could wait.

Jake hissed in his breath. His expression was stony, his eyes blue ice, unreadable. 'You swore to me when I came back from the Amazon that he wasn't my child.' Each word bit into her. 'You reminded me that you'd been on the pill when we made love…that one and only time. When I asked how you fell pregnant if you were on the pill, you told me you'd stopped taking it after I left. That you'd turned to Dominic because you thought I'd left you for good.'

His lip curled. 'You swore to me that your child was conceived a full month after I left. And that as soon as you found out, and told Dominic, he insisted on marrying you right away.'

Red spots stained her cheeks. 'It—it wasn't like that, Jake. I had to tell you that because I was married to Dominic by then. I—I wasn't on the pill when you made love to me. I've never been on the pill. I only told you I was because—' She bit her lip, then ploughed on. 'Because I could see how concerned you were about—about not having taken precautions. About leaving me with the—

160

the possible consequences. I was afraid you'd worry about it when you were on the Amazon and not concentrate on what you were doing. I—I never thought—' She let her hands flutter helplessly in the air.

'Didn't you, Lexie?' His scathing tone chilled her to the bone. 'Maybe you were hoping that if I *had* made you pregnant I'd—'

'No, Jake! No!' she denied hotly. 'If I'd planned it, don't you think I'd have sent word to you the moment I knew I was expecting your child? And tried to bring you back home?'

'Why didn't you?' His eyes narrowed. 'You think I wouldn't have come home the first moment I could? Wouldn't have wanted my own child?' Before she could answer he rasped, 'Could the truth be that you *knew* I wouldn't be fooled? Your baby arrived ten months after I left, remember, not *nine* months. In my book, that means I *can't* be the father!'

'But you are, Jake! We—Dominic and I—we told everyone the baby was due a—a month later than it really was! And when Sam was born nearly four weeks late...babies often *are* late—everyone just assumed he'd arrived on time.'

She drew in a tremulous breath. 'I'd lost a lot of weight after you left and—and nobody even knew I was pregnant until several months into the pregnancy. I didn't put on much weight all the way through. Only my doctor knew Sam's real birth date.

'Jake, I didn't make love to Dominic until *after* he married me. Honestly. He *was* a big comfort to me after you left, that's true, but that was all he was. A comforting shoulder to lean on. He knew I wasn't in love with him. I—I loved him as a brother...as a friend...but not—not in that way. Not the way I loved you.'

'And yet you married him,' Jake bit out. 'And would still be married to him now, still be making out that Sam was his child, if Dominic was still alive.'

She shook her head, gulping in a fractured breath. She wouldn't have been with Dominic today…but she couldn't go into that now. 'Jake…Dominic knew I didn't love him the—the way I loved you, but he insisted it would be enough, that I'd grow to love him more in time. He'd always been good and kind to me, Jake, a dependable, home-loving, family-oriented man. I knew he'd look after Sam and me. Be a good husband and father.'

She shivered slightly. 'I married him, Jake, for Sam's sake. To give my child a stable, secure family life, the kind of life that I'd never had. With the security of having two parents who would love him and always be there for him.' And it had been like that too…in the beginning.

Jake shook off her hand and stepped back, away from her, as if he couldn't bear to touch her. 'You think I wouldn't have given him those things?' His scorn lashed her. 'Before I went off to the Amazon, you swore that you loved me, that you would always love me. And yet you couldn't even wait two years for me to come back! You didn't even try to contact me, or give me the *chance* to come back any sooner than I did!'

She felt panic in her heart, and tried to explain. 'You said any distractions could be dangerous, remember? And as for me not waiting, you didn't *ask* me to wait. You talked vaguely about taking me with you on future assignments as a *working* partner, but never about wanting to settle down, never about loving me or wanting a family.'

She lifted pained eyes to his. 'I knew that even if you did come back one day it wouldn't be to stay. I knew you'd hate being tied down, that you'd feel trapped knowing you had a child. You'd have felt you had no *choice* but to stay. I—I didn't want to put you in that position, Jake!'

She rushed on before he could speak. 'Anyway, by the time I found out I was pregnant nobody even knew where you were. We hadn't heard a word. But Dominic was there for me, offering what I knew you never would, never could. At that time I wanted—needed—a man I could rely on, Jake. A man who would be there for me and my child all the time!'

She bowed her head, her hair a midnight veil round her face. 'Jake, please try to understand.' It was a bleak plea. 'Put yourself in my place. What else was I to do…or think? You went off, not knowing how long you'd be gone or even if you'd be back. You let me think I had no future with you, not the kind of future I'd always longed for.

'It was a shock when—after two years without a single word from you—you breezed back, out of the blue, expecting me to be waiting, ready to fall into your arms. But you never intended to stay, did you, Jake? Try being honest yourself. You've never wanted to settle down in one place…you never will!'

Jake gave a frustrated jerk of his head. 'You weren't thinking of settling down either…when I left five years ago. Hell, Lexie, you were only twenty-one! You were still studying, still a cadet journalist. We were talking about travelling the world together one day, working as partners—'

'I said I wanted that because I *loved* you, Jake, and saw it as the only way to be with you! But when I realised I was expecting a child it changed everything. I had to put my child's needs first.'

'And my needs or wishes didn't matter?' Jake sucked in his breath. 'I couldn't send word to you,' he grated. 'I warned you I might not be able to. Besides, I wanted you to get on with your life, concentrate on your career, your studies, feel free to live your life. Hell, I didn't even know if I'd survive to see you again!'

He heaved a deep sigh. 'I came back as soon as I could. I was *missing* you, dammit. I was burning to see you again, to hold you again, to find out if you still cared about me. The last thing I expected was to find you'd married my wimpy cousin, only weeks after I'd left—and that you had a baby over a year old. Naturally I was suspicious. But when I questioned you you looked me straight in the eye and told me the child was Dominic's. And you made me believe it!'

'Jake, what else could I do?' Her eyes pleaded with him. 'Dominic was my husband by then, bringing up Sam as his own child. He—he was adamant that we didn't tell a soul. He felt that since he was a blood relative, Sam's uncle by blood, nobody would ever know or guess.' A shiver rippled down her spine.

'Jake, what did you expect me to do?' she cried hoarsely. 'Wait until you came back from wherever you were, shove Sam under your nose, and demand that you marry me and stay at home for our child's sake? Even if I hadn't expected anything of you, you'd have felt you *had* to do the right thing. And you'd have ended up resenting us both after a while; you'd have become bitter and frustrated about what you'd had to give up—you know you would!'

'You never even gave me a choice!' There was still no softening in his voice. But his eyes…was that a faint glimmer in the blue depths?

'Jake, it wasn't only that…' She pressed on shakily, wanting Jake to know everything. 'I had no money, no husband, no home or family of my own. I was scared that you or—or Bonnie and Cliff might try to talk me into giving my baby up, giving him over to married parents who could give him a proper home, a proper family life—'

'You truly believed that Bonnie and Cliff wouldn't have supported you?' Jake cut in, his tone derisive. 'Wouldn't have wanted to help you out?'

'Jake, they both work, they're busy people, and they're not young. I was so afraid that they—that they might not *want* to have a baby in the house. I'm not even their real daughter! I—I didn't know what to do. Dominic seemed my only way out. He was offering me the kind of life I'd always dreamed—foolishly—of having one day with *you*, Jake…a home, security, a family of my own. And he loved me. You never even told me until tonight, Jake, that you loved me. Not even when you made love to me that time!'

Jake heaved a sigh, his eyes dark hollows in his face, his jaw tense, the small distance between them still a gaping chasm. 'When I went off to the Amazon it was far too soon to talk about love and commitment. I wanted you to feel *free*, not leave you feeling emotionally tied to me when I didn't even know if I'd ever see you again. It was one hell of a shock when I came back two years later and found that you obviously hadn't missed me at all! Or not for long…' He paused. 'Or that's how it looked to me at the time.'

As her lips parted, he shook his head. 'No…let me finish.' His face was still taut. 'I didn't care what happened to me after that. I just wanted to keep away from you. Away from Australia. I took on the most dangerous assignments going to blot you out of my mind, my life. Between assignments, I tackled some of the most dangerous rivers in the world. Anything to avoid coming home, seeing you again, seeing you with my smug, smirking cousin. I stayed away until I heard that Dominic had been killed in an accident at the plant…'

'You mean you came back because—' She hesitated, hardly daring to say it.

'I came back,' he admitted, his voice softening for the first time, 'because I knew there would never be another woman for me but you, Lexie. I had to find out if there was anything still there between us, if there could ever be another chance for us. But you'd just been widowed, and I was only back for a brief visit. It wasn't the right time to tell you how I felt about you. And there was still a lot of bitterness, a lot to be resolved between us.'

He paused, looking down at her with eyes that held a more tender glitter now. 'I sensed you still felt something for me, but I wasn't sure...just what. I needed to know that you wanted me, loved me, for what and who I am...for the *way* I am, wherever in the world I happen to be...that you weren't just looking for a replacement for Dominic, and hoping that I might have changed enough to fill the gap he'd left in your life.'

'Oh, Jake!' She gave a muffled cry. 'I'd never want another Dominic...ever! I was—' She broke off abruptly, her head whipping round. Shrill screams were coming from the room opposite.

Her heart went cold. 'Something's wrong with Sam!' She flew across the passage to her son's room, sensing Jake's silent presence close behind.

The child was thrashing about in his bed, shouting, 'No! No! Don't! Please don't! Stop it! *Please* don't!'

'He's having a nightmare,' she cried. As she bent over the bed, Sam screamed, '*No*, Daddy! You can't! No! Give it back! *No-o-o!*' he moaned, and started pummelling the air with his tiny fists. 'I hate you, I hate you, I hate you!'

The blood drained from Lexie's face as she caught the boy's tiny body in her arms. 'Sam, baby, wake up! It's just a dream. It's all right, darling, nobody's taking anything from you. You've been having a bad dream.'

The child shuddered, and blinked up at her. 'Mummy! Mummy!' He wound his arms round her neck and clung to her. 'But he *did*, Mummy! He took my pictures away and tore them all up! He tore up Uncle Jake's picture too!'

'Oh, darling...' She couldn't look at Jake, standing so still and silent behind her. 'Daddy's sorry for that. Truly sorry.' She bit her lip. 'Darling, Jake has another copy of that magazine for you, with those same elephant pictures. You remember him showing them to you? He's minding them for you.'

'You bet I am,' Jake put in gently. But his face was inscrutable. 'It's yours, tiger, whenever you—'

'No!' Sam shook his head violently. 'Daddy said—Daddy said—'

'Oh, baby...' Lexie hugged him. 'Daddy didn't mean to be unkind. He lost his temper. He's sorry now for what he did. He'd *want* you to have Jake's elephant pictures. Daddy loved you, Sam...he loved both of us.'

'No, he didn't!' the child choked out, his voice muffled against her shoulder. 'He didn't love *me*. He didn't!'

'Oh, darling, yes, he did. He loved you very much. He never meant to make you unhappy, darling. He had a—a lot on his mind and it made him lash out at people and do and say things he was sorry about later. He was angry with *himself*, darling, not with you.'

She gulped, aware of Jake listening to every word. 'Daddy's in heaven now, darling...he's not cross any more. He's happy again, the way he used to be. You remember the way he used to be, don't you, darling?' she asked softly. 'Remember when he used to take you to the beach? And for picnics? And give you rides at the playground?'

Sam chewed on his lip. 'I *think* I 'member.' He gazed

up at her with his big dark eyes. 'D-Daddy doesn't hate me any more? He's not cross any more, now he's in heaven?'

'Of course he doesn't hate you, dear. He never hated you,' she assured him, her heart twisting. Dominic had hated himself, and maybe Jake, but not Jake's child. 'He didn't mean to be so bad-tempered and cross, pet. He just…wasn't himself. But he's not cross any more. He's smiling down at both of us.' One day, she thought, I'll explain to you, Sam. When you're old enough to understand.

'Here, drink some of this,' she said, reaching for the glass of water beside his bed. She held it as he gulped a few mouthfuls. 'That's a good boy.' She stroked his brow, feeling its clammy warmth, thankfully nothing like the raging heat of earlier. 'Go back to sleep, precious. You'll be all right now…Mummy's right here.'

'And Uncle Jake?' Sam whispered, his gaze fluttering past her.

'I'm right here, tiger.' Jake's soft voice curled past her. 'You can go back to sleep now, son. We're right here.'

'Son.' The word quivered through Lexie. She turned her head and sought his gaze, holding it for a long, throbbing moment. 'I'll stay until he's asleep,' she breathed.

'Here…put this over you.' Jake picked up a crocheted rug from the foot of the bed and draped it over her shoulders. 'When he's asleep, go and get some sleep yourself, Lexie. I'll be in the spare room. We'll both be able to hear him if he wakes.'

She nodded, swallowing hard. His eyes were telling her that tomorrow he would have some questions he would want answered.

before. He never attacked Sam, or anything like that,
never struck him—'

She swallowed, her fingers curling round her mug. 'Late
afternoon that one day, before he rang, she got to Sam, in a
blind panic, scooped him up and—and ran off.... She begged
Dominic never to hurt Sam.... Dominic. The words were
not—'

CHAPTER THIRTEEN

IT WAS almost lunchtime before they had a chance to talk.
With Amy popping in to see how Sam was, and Sam's
needs to be dealt with, there hadn't been a spare moment
until now. But now the boy was asleep again, and Jake,
having made some fresh coffee, was steering her purpose-
fully into the lounge. He waved her to a chair and pulled
one up for himself, facing hers.

She took a sip of her coffee, watching him warily over
the rim of her mug.

'Now...' Jake leaned back in his armchair, but his expression was far less relaxed than his lithe, long-legged
frame, his face tight, mouth grim, blue eyes glinting with
hard intent. 'What's this about Dominic losing his temper
and tearing up Sam's pictures? What was going on, Lexie?
Why was my son so frightened of him?' A sardonic curve
twisted his lips. 'For all my cousin's shortcomings, I would
never have taken him for the violent type.'

'Oh, Jake, he wasn't. It was just that he—that when he
saw that article of yours with the picture of *you* in it, and
saw how Sam was poring over it, utterly fascinated by it,
by *you*, he—something seemed to snap, and he went right
off his head. He grabbed it and tore it into tiny pieces, in
front of Sam. He was so—' she gulped '—so afraid, so
paranoid that his parents or friends would see a likeness
between Sam and *you*, Jake—the same look, the same
mannerisms, or even the same love of photography, or
travel, or adventure—and start putting two and two to-

gether. He—he never attacked Sam or anything like that, never *hit* him, but—'

She wavered, her fingers curling round her mug. 'I was afraid that one day he—he *might* lash out at Sam, in a blind rage, and do him some real harm.' She raised haunted dark eyes to Jake's. 'Dominic's black moods were getting worse each day. I tried to get him to seek help, but he wouldn't—he got mad at the very suggestion. He'd changed so much, Jake. When we were first married he was so—so gentle and contented and loving, so sure we were doing the right thing...' She trailed off with a mournful shake of her head.

'There are to be no more secrets between us, Lexie,' Jake said quietly, yet with an iron firmness in his tone. 'I want you to tell me everything. Everything...' His eyes compelled hers. 'When did you first notice that Dominic had changed? Was it around the time I came back from the Amazon?'

Her fingers played nervously with the mug in her hand. She took a deep breath. 'I...guess so,' she admitted tentatively. 'Even though you left very quickly, Jake, and didn't have much to say—at least, not to him,' she said, gulping at the memory of her own heated clash with Jake, 'he knew that seeing you again had...unsettled me.'

Her tongue flicked over her lips. 'Do you remember the way you kissed me, Jake, before you left three years ago? You were mad at me for marrying Dominic so soon after you'd gone away. You seemed to want to hurt me, to—to punish me for what I'd done to you. You kissed me with a—with a ferocity, a wildness I'd never seen in you before. And then you snapped at me, "Remember *that* when you're in bed with that insipid cousin of mine!" I—I hated you in that moment. But I...I did remember it, Jake. I couldn't help it. It brought back all the feelings I'd been trying so hard to forget, to deny to myself that I'd ever had.'

'That was my intention,' Jake said roughly. 'I wanted you to suffer the way I was suffering. I'm sorry, Lexie...' his tone gentled '...if it made things worse for you...with Dominic. You told him, I suppose?'

'No!' she denied at once. 'He was jealous enough of you already. But what worried him most about your visit was that you might have seen something of yourself in Sam—some likeness—when you asked to see him.' She drew in a wavery breath. 'He started imagining that other people would see a likeness too, and guess the truth, and sneer at him behind his back.

'It got worse later on when I failed to fall pregnant. For a long time he blamed *me*...even after my doctor confirmed that there was no medical reason to stop me having another child.' She paused to gulp a mouthful of her coffee.

Jake's lip curled. 'He would.' His eyes narrowed, searching hers. Then he said slowly, 'There's something you're not telling me. What is it, Lexie? Dominic thought you didn't *want* his child? Was that it?'

Her gaze fluttered away. 'He—he preferred to blame anything rather than face the possibility that it might be some fault in himself.' She sighed. 'I managed in the end to persuade him to have some tests done. I said it might be some simple thing that could be fixed. But the tests revealed that he couldn't *have* children, and that nothing could be done about it. It came as a terrible shock to him, as you can imagine. To both of us.'

A shadow crossed her face. 'Dominic never got over it. He was so afraid it would leak out somehow and that everyone would *know* then that Sam wasn't his child. He started to get really paranoid about it, Jake. He got more and more touchy and morose. In the end, his dark moods got so bad that even his family noticed.'

She shivered. 'It was as if he had demons inside him, tormenting him, turning his gentle nature into something sour and—and warped. He became so bitter and self-pitying, haunted by imaginary fears. I—I tried to tell him that only his own behaviour would make people guess the truth, that they'd never hear it from *me*. Or from our doctor, who was the only other person who knew. He said...'

'Yes, Lexie?' Jake pressed gently as she paused. 'Tell me.'

She repressed a shudder. 'He said, "*Sam* will know! It's only a matter of time. And one of these days bloody Jake will find out!"'

She gulped down the remains of her coffee, then looked up with bleak dark eyes. 'Jake, I was so afraid that Dominic would snap one day and take out his frustration on Sam. After seeing his blind fury the day he tore up Sam's magazine, I was petrified that eventually he'd lose control completely and do something really bad to Sam. I wasn't going to risk that. And so I—I made up my mind to leave him. I could see no other way.'

'You were going to *leave* Dominic? Leave your *home*?' Jake stared at her. 'You were actually going to walk out on your marriage and the security that meant so much to you? Even if it meant bringing up your son on your own?'

'Jake...' She gave a poignant half-smile. 'I know that at one time all I dreamed of was having a home and a family of my own. Security. Stability. *Roots*. But, Jake, none of those things mean much if you're married to the wrong person. Or if you're afraid. I realised when Dominic lost his temper with Sam that day that all that mattered was my son's safety and well-being. It wouldn't be easy, I knew that...leaving my husband and starting a new life on my own, with a small child. It would have meant leaving Bonnie and Cliff too, of course. They—'

'You think they'd have let you go out of their lives?' Jake scoffed. 'You've been a daughter to them from the moment you first came into their home!'

She flinched at the scorn in his voice. 'Once Dominic told them *why* I'd left him—because Sam wasn't his real son, or their grandson—do you honestly believe they'd have wanted to keep in touch with me? They'd have sided with Dominic, their son…naturally. No…I knew I'd be on my own, apart from Sam, that I'd be leaving with nothing. Nothing but some catering expertise and a small amount of money I'd managed to save from working in partnership with Bonnie.

'But I knew I had to go. Not just for Sam's sake, but for Dominic's sake too. With us out of his life, he had some chance of going back to the way he used to be.'

'Poor Lexie.' Jake leaned forward in his chair and plucked her mug from her fingers, putting it down beside his. Then he caught her hands in his. 'Did Dominic have any idea that you were planning to leave him?'

'I—I never had a chance to tell him. Maybe if I had…' She faltered. 'Maybe the prospect of losing us both might have jolted him out of his morbid self-pity. But I doubt it.' She shook her head sadly. 'He was so paranoid and panicky by then…so convinced that someone was going to guess at any moment that Sam wasn't his child…and so much in dread of *you* coming back again one day, Jake…'

She drew in a deep, trembling breath. 'I—I'm sure he sensed that I was still in love with you, Jake, even though I tried so hard to convince him—and myself—that I wasn't, that I…hated you.'

'Love and hate are often pretty much the same emotion,'

Jake said with a brief, ironic smile. 'For three years I tried to fool myself that I hated you too.'

'Oh, Jake…you had good reason to hate me!' Even more reason now that he knew she'd denied him his son for so long. 'Five years ago, Jake,' she confessed shakily, 'when you went off to the Amazon and I found myself pregnant, I was so immature and foolish. I thought you'd left me for good, believed Dominic when he said you'd just—just used me, that you would never care about me or my baby. I imagined that *he* could give me the stable, secure, happy family life and home I wanted my child to have, that I'd never had and had always longed for. I was so terribly wrong!'

Shining strands of black hair fell across her cheeks as she bowed her head, her body trembling. She heard a sound and looked up to see Jake kneeling in front of her. He raised her hands to his lips and kissed her.

'You did the best you could, Lexie. You mustn't blame yourself for what happened to Dominic. He married you and took on our child with his eyes wide open. He loved you and was prepared to have you any way he could. It's not your fault he changed, fell into a black pit. His own personal demons were responsible for that.'

Still on his knees, he slipped his arms round her, cradling her against his chest. 'You must put it all behind you now, Lexie. Dominic would want you to. For all his faults, he did love you…I'll say that for him. And I don't think for a minute he would ever have done anything to harm Sam. Or anybody…anybody but himself. He never was the physically dangerous type. Inner torment was always more his style.'

'Poor Dominic,' Lexie whispered shakily. Suddenly her eyes leapt to his. 'Jake…maybe he didn't trip on those stairs at work…maybe he *threw* himself down them…to put an end to his misery!' She shuddered, her dark gaze stark under his. 'I can't help wondering…if I'd walked out on him earlier…if I hadn't waited…'

'You mustn't think like that, Lexie!' Jake's tone was harsh. 'Walking out on him might have plunged him even deeper into the black pit he was in. Who's to say what a warped mind will make a man do? He always did have a weak, gutless streak, Dominic.'

'But it might have been a *relief* to him, Jake, having me out of his life, knowing that the truth about Sam could come out at last. He could have blamed *me*…and maybe in time even started a new life with…somebody else.'

'Dominic?' Jake gave a snort. 'I doubt that. He was besotted with you, Lexie. Obsessed. Always was. Knowing he'd lost you for good might have tipped him over the edge completely.' He paused, adding with a touch of irony, 'I always knew how he felt about you, Lexie, but, stupidly, I never worried about him moving in on you in my absence, because I never thought *you'd* be interested in him…not in that way.'

'Jake, I never was—' she began, but he hushed her with a finger to her lips.

'I know that now, my darling. And I understand why you married him. You were thinking of the child you were carrying. And of what *you'd* missed out on as a child. It's all right, Lexie,' he said with a softness that wrenched at her heart. 'It all makes sense to me now. You never have to worry about it again. It's over. It's behind us.'

Still on his knees, he stretched his neck to brush his lips over hers. 'You must look to the future now, my love. For Sam's sake. And yours. And, dammit, for mine too.'

'Oh, Jake.' She brought her hand up to stroke his rough cheek with tender fingers. 'Are you saying you forgive me for what I did? For—'

'Hush,' he said. 'There's nothing to forgive. And I can't tell you how happy and proud I am to know that Sam is my son. Our son. From now on, my darling Lexie, you and I are going to look ahead, not back, do you hear? And we're going to be together, you and Sam and I. I'm not going to risk losing you again.'

As she caught her breath in shocked wonder, he took her hand in his. 'Will you do me the honour of marrying me, my dearest love? And you'd better answer me quick smart,' he groaned, screwing up his face, 'before my knees pack up and I can never straighten them again!'

Her eyes widened to deep pools of blazing ebony. 'You want to *marry* me, Jake?' A smile trembled on her lips, part disbelief, part amusement, at the anguished look on his face. And total joy. Then, wavering, she said, 'You…you're not just—'

'Just say yes or no!' he grated, his strong, sun-bronzed face contorting in agony.

'Yes!' Her answer burst from her. She wasn't going to lose her chance. Never again.

Jake beamed, then growled, 'Now come here!' He pulled her down beside him on the carpet, letting out another groan as he painfully unfolded his long legs and stretched them out in front of him. 'Now…let's seal our contract with a kiss,' he suggested, wrapping her in his arms.

She joyously lifted her face to his, her lips parting, full and ready. It was some time before either of them spoke again, before either was capable of speaking.

'Jake…' At long last, lying nestled in the warmth of his shoulder, feeling happier than she had ever felt before in her life, she broached more practical matters. 'If you think I'm going to expect you to give up your overseas assignments, my wonderful, adventure-loving hero, I'm not,' she said firmly. 'I know what your work means to you...what your freedom of movement means to you...'

Glancing up at him, she saw something stir deep in his eyes.

'Lexie, I love my work, I love taking photographs; I won't deny that.' His voice was a soft purr that brushed over her like warm velvet. 'But the assignments I've chosen to take on in the past three years have been more a substitute than anything...a way of blotting *you* from my mind. Knowing I'd lost you. Thinking I'd lost you for good. Not caring if I lived or died.'

He looked deep into her eyes, stroking her face with gentle fingers. 'If I take on any overseas assignments in the future—and I say *if*—I'll be choosing ones that won't put my neck in jeopardy or keep me away from you and Sam for long. But I'm not envisaging leaving Australia in the foreseeable future. There are limitless possibilities right here in this great country of ours. From now on, my dearest one, I want a permanent home base...a family...a loving wife in my arms at night. And I want to help you raise our fine, healthy son.'

Her heart soared with sheer happiness. But as the word 'healthy' hit her she gave a tiny cry, and raised her head. 'I should check on Sam.'

'Check on him if you like, Lexie,' Jake said calmly. 'But I'd say he's still sleeping soundly, if that snoring I can hear from his room is anything to go by.'

She listened hard for a second, and then smiled up at him in relief. And amazement. 'Fancy you hearing that, Jake. I can barely hear it myself. It just shows how much of a bond there is between the two of you already.' The thought brought a warm prickle to the back of her eyes. 'Sam loves you, Jake. Adores you. He took to you quicker than he's ever taken to anybody else, ever.'

She felt a fleeting stab of regret that it had taken so long for Jake to get to know his son. But she was going to make up for that. Jake didn't know yet what she had decided.

'He was already intrigued by you, Jake, and by your photographs, before he even got to know you,' she told him huskily. 'Dominic was right about that.' She found, to her relief, that at last she could talk about Dominic without the old pain and guilt. It was as if he'd been laid to rest at last.

'Lexie…I know how much you love this house you're living in,' Jake said, brushing her hair back from her face, 'but it's going to be too small for us, I'm afraid. I'm going to need a good-sized studio…and a darkroom…and I think we should have a bigger garden and more bedrooms if we're going to have more kids.'

More kids. Her heart felt as if it would burst. 'You'd really like more children, Jake?'

'Of course.' He glanced at her. 'Wouldn't you?'

'Yes, of course.' Her face shone, her eyes bright as stars. 'But…we needn't rush into it, Jake. You have your big Australian book to work on after you've finished your Sydney assignment. That will take some time, you said.'

'Oh, that!' Jake was dismissive. 'I can start work on that later. When I do, I'll still need a home base to work from. I intend to do the book in dribs and drabs, a city or a state at a time, coming back home in between…even if it takes longer that way. I don't want to be away from you and Sam for any longer than I have to.

'But before I start work on that…' he kissed the tip of her nose '…I want to spend a bit longer here at home, with you and my son. It's what I intended all along…I just didn't want to tell you before I knew how *you* really felt.'

She smiled mistily up at him, elation filling her heart. Now was the time to tell him.

'But you will be with us, Jake. Or we'll be with you. Sam and I will be coming with you when you travel around Australia taking photographs for your book,' she announced smugly, watching his face. 'We could hire a camper van or take a four-wheel drive and tents, and travel around the country like gypsies. That way, we'll be seeing the country together. *Being* together. Even working together, if you want any help from me.'

He stared at her in amazement. 'You'd *want* to do that? Uproot yourselves to travel around Australia for months on end? Taking Sam away from the safe, settled environment that's always been so important to you? Is it what *you* want for yourself, Lexie?' he asked, frowning. 'It would mean roughing it for a good deal of the time—becoming a footloose nomad for the duration. And it would mean giving up your cooking job and your dining-out column. That wouldn't matter to me—you've no need to go on working—but if you enjoy it...'

'Jake, I'm not worried about giving up baking cakes for a living,' she said flatly. 'And, as I told you before, the dining-out column is only a fill-in job until Sarah gets back, which will be in two weeks' time. And I'm certainly not worried about roughing it. I'd love it...travelling around. So would Sam. As long as we're together, the three of us.

'Home, Jake, is where your loved ones are. It's not brick walls. It's not a safe, secure roof over your head. I've learned that much in the past five years. I'll make a home for you, Jake—for the three of us—when we travel around Australia together.'

She flashed a bright smile at Jake, who was looking bemused. 'And don't worry about the demise of my so-called cooking career,' she said breezily. 'I only took it on to give myself an income…and some independence. I'd much rather be writing—poems, children's stories, feature articles. And I could be thinking about those, or jotting down ideas, while we're travelling around. It will give me something to do while you're working. Maybe I'll even end up selling something one day.'

'My…you have it all worked out, haven't you?' Jake said admiringly, some deep emotion bringing a breath-catching shimmer to his eyes. She knew what that look meant. He knew now, without any doubt, that she wanted him for himself—loved and wanted him for the man he was, no matter where in the world he happened to be—and that he wouldn't just be filling a gap in her life, a need that Dominic's death had left.

That was why he'd held back in the past…not because he'd wanted to go on living his dangerous, footloose life in remote corners of the world, not because he was against settling down, but because he'd needed to be sure that she loved him for himself, and that she would love and want him no matter what kind of life he led, at home or away.

'Well, now…' Jake's voice broke into her thoughts. 'I have an even better idea.'

She searched his face, her hands itching to grab his head and pull his face down to hers so that she could press her lips to his all over again.

'What?' she asked cautiously. He didn't want her up-rooting Sam…was that it? He was about to let her down lightly, dissuade her from going away with him. He wanted to be independent…to feel free to work on his own, to move around on his own. The way he'd always done.

She would have to accept it. She *would* accept it. Whatever Jake wanted.

When he answered it was a moment before his words sank in.

'Become my partner in the book, Lexie. Write the text for me. And if any of my photographs happen to particularly inspire you compose poems to go with them. We'll make it a joint production.'

A joyous breath caught in her throat. 'Oh, Jake, do you mean it?' Her brow cleared, a rapturous light in her eyes. It was what she had always longed for—back in the days when she had still had dreams. To work alongside Jake, the two of them producing articles and books together. Doing everything together…for always.

'You can still write your children's stories…there'll be time for those when we're back home again, bringing up our tribe of kids…together. I've done with all that endless, uncomfortable, dismally lonely travelling, Lexie,' he assured her, dropping a kiss on her brow. 'Being away from home for months and years on end, taking on the most dangerous assignments I could lay my hands on, with barely a break in between. Risking my neck and not even caring. It's out of my system now, believe me…'

She gazed up at him, still finding it hard to believe what he was saying. 'Jake, I'd never try to—' she began, but he stopped her with a kiss.

'You still don't believe I mean it, do you, my darling? I do. I've had more than my share of Amazons…the first would have been enough, if I could have had you. I have a chance for a new life now, a chance I thought I'd lost for ever. And it's going to be a better, happier, far more fulfilling life than the half-life I've been living these past years.'

He paused to smile down at her, a tender brilliance in his eyes. 'Besides, these days I value my neck too much. And I value my family above all, Lexie…you and Sam.

From now on we're going to do everything we can together. If I have to be away from home for more than a few days, we'll go together. We'll take our holidays together. And, above all, we'll enjoy being at home... together.'

She still could hardly believe she was hearing the words, the words she'd longed to hear, imagined in her dreams so long ago.

'Jake,' she breathed, brushing a wayward lock of brown hair back from his brow. 'I never thought I'd ever be this happy. I thought I'd messed up my life for ever. And Sam's too.'

He pressed his lips briefly to hers. 'We'll make up for the time we've missed out on, Lexie. You and I have been given a second chance, my darling.' He drew back sharply, as if he'd heard something. 'Sam's awake,' he said. 'I can hear him making grunting noises.'

'Jake, you're amazing!' she cried, only now hearing the sounds too. 'Your years of dicing with death and danger must have given you superhuman hearing.'

She pulled down his head and kissed him, a quick, hard kiss, then scrambled to her feet, tugging him up with her.

'Let's see how he is. If he's feeling better, Jake, shall we tell him that his uncle Jake is going to be his new daddy? It's what he's been hoping for, Jake,' she told him, a joyful tremor in her voice. 'You—you don't mind that he doesn't know the whole truth yet?' she asked hesitantly. 'It—it might be a bit soon...to explain it all...'

'Far too soon,' Jake agreed. 'Let him get used to having me around for a while. As a permanent fixture. As his new daddy. Then, later, when he's old enough to understand, we'll tell him that I'm his real father. We'll tell him together.'

Together. That magical word again. She smiled up into

his tough, bronzed face, her heart bursting with sheer happiness. And it was together, with Jake's arm firmly clasped round her waist and his warmth and strength flowing through her, that they told Sam that they were going to be a family, the three of them, and that they would be looking for a new, bigger house to live in, with a bigger garden for him to play in, and lots of bedrooms so that they could give him a brother or a sister one day.

Sam's recovery after that was miraculous.

163   ELIZABETH DUKE

EPILOGUE

EIGHTEEN months later a daughter, a cherished young sister for Sam, was born. Lexie and Jake had conceived Stephanie during their camper-van tour of Australia, and she was born only a month after their return. She had inherited her father's piercing blue eyes and the blonde curls he himself had had as a child.

Early the following year, Jake and Lexie Thorn's book, *Australia—the Human Face*, was launched in the garden of their spacious family home near the Hawkesbury river north of Sydney. Cliff Thorn made a speech, and Bonnie Thorn did the catering, putting on a truly magnificent spread.

A proud Sam Thorn read aloud one of his mother's poems from the book.

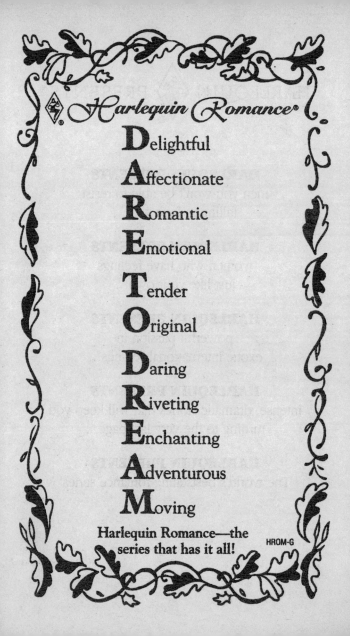

Harlequin Romance®

Delightful

Affectionate

Romantic

Emotional

Tender

Original

Daring

Riveting

Enchanting

Adventurous

Moving

Harlequin Romance—the
series that has it all!

HROM-G

HARLEQUIN 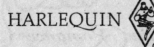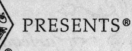 PRESENTS®

HARLEQUIN PRESENTS
men you won't be able to resist
falling in love with...

HARLEQUIN PRESENTS
women who have feelings
just like your own...

HARLEQUIN PRESENTS
powerful passion in
exotic international settings...

HARLEQUIN PRESENTS
intense, dramatic stories that will keep you
turning to the very last page...

HARLEQUIN PRESENTS
The world's bestselling romance series!

♦ Harlequin®
Historical

From rugged lawmen and
valiant knights to defiant heiresses
and spirited frontierswomen,
Harlequin Historicals will
capture your imagination with
their dramatic scope, passion
and adventure.

Harlequin Historicals...
they're too good to miss!

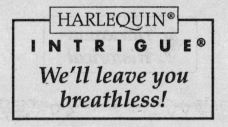

LOOK FOR OUR FOUR FABULOUS MEN!

Each month some of today's bestselling authors bring
four new fabulous men to Harlequin American Romance.
Whether they're rebel ranchers, millionaire power brokers
or sexy single dads, they're all gallant princes—and
they're all ready to sweep you into lighthearted fantasies
and contemporary fairy tales where anything is possible
and where all your dreams come true!

You don't even have to make a wish...
Harlequin American Romance will grant your every desire!

Look for Harlequin American Romance
wherever Harlequin books are sold!

HARLEQUIN SUPERROMANCE®

...there's more to the story!

Superromance. A *big* satisfying read about unforgettable characters. Each month we offer *four* very different stories that range from family drama to adventure and mystery, from highly emotional stories to romantic comedies—and much more! Stories about people you'll believe in and care about. Stories too compelling to put down....

Our authors are among today's *best* romance writers. You'll find familiar names and talented newcomers. Many of them are award winners—and you'll see why!

If you want the biggest and best in romance fiction, you'll get it from Superromance!

Available wherever Harlequin books are sold.

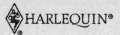

Not The Same Old Story!

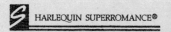

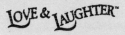